Doctor's Date with a Billionaire

Pittsburgh

DOCTOR'S DATE WITH A BILLIONAIRE

ANJ Press, First edition. MAY 2019.

Copyright © 2019 Amelia Addler.

Written by Amelia Addler.

Cover design by Charmaine Ross at CharmaineRoss.com

For Nate
my thoughtful, funny, handsome, silly, strong husband.
I'm lucky that the dog rested his head on your chest
all those years ago to let me know
that you were a good guy.
You are more amazing than anyone I could dream up.

Chapter 1

Jason looked at his watch and sighed. His dad was late, as usual. He tried to focus on the menu and decide on lunch, but he kept catching himself looking around the restaurant instead; he was worried he'd been followed.

Nobody looked suspicious, and truth be told, he didn't know what he would do if there *was* someone suspicious. It made him nervous nevertheless.

After what felt like an eternity, Marty "Make it Happen" Brash finally arrived.

"Sorry I'm late," his dad said in a low voice. "I have to be extra careful these days."

Marty was out on bail, and in a few short weeks he would stand trial to answer for decades of financial crimes and fraud.

"It's okay."

Jason wasn't sure how to feel. Part of him hoped that his dad wouldn't show up to lunch. Then the only time he'd have to face him would be at trial.

"What's new with you?" Marty asked, sitting back casually.

What an absurd question. They hadn't seen each other in three years, yet he acted like they were just catching up.

Jason decided that it was best not to drag it out. "There are some things I need to tell you."

Marty peered down at his menu. "How's work?"

"It's fine," Jason said, crossing him arms. "Nothing exciting." He couldn't stand faking pleasant conversation with his dad, pretending that everything was okay.

Marty continued. "What's good here? Do you think the turkey burgers are decent? I'm supposed to watch my cholesterol."

"I'm not really sure."

"What lonely soul even came up with turkey burgers?" his dad mused.

Now Jason knew that he was stalling on purpose. "There's something I think you deserve to know. You've hurt a lot of people. And I've agreed to testify against you at trial."

Marty didn't react right away. He kept looking at the choices in front of him, eyes scanning back and forth. After a moment, he set the menu down. "I know, son."

Jason sat back, surprised. He'd dreaded having to say that out loud for the past few weeks – no, actually it was a dread he'd had for years.

When he was younger, he didn't realize that his father was actually a conman. At first, Jason was even unwittingly part of his father's schemes.

It started when he was in high school when his dad needed help with the computer.

"There are always problems with these computers," he'd say. "How am I supposed to get anything done?"

Jason showed him how to use a word processor and spreadsheets to keep track of things, including expenses, payments, and business partners.

Jason had no idea what any of the numbers or names were linked to. At that age, he didn't quite understand what fraud was. He didn't know that his dad was the go-to guy for white collar crime. All he knew was that it took his dad forever to do anything on the computer, so he had to keep track of everything for him.

As he got older, Jason learned that none of his dad's businesses or banking deals were legitimate. He quickly removed himself from anything to do with the "family business." He was ashamed that he was ever involved. After dropping out of college, Jason got an apprenticeship as a carpenter. He never looked back.

It wasn't until FBI agents showed up at his door that he truly understood the stunning depths of his dad's crimes. Jason wasn't in any trouble, and while that was good news for him, it made the agents worry it was a long shot that he'd say anything against his father.

When they showed him how much money his father stole, and how much it hurt innocent people who were too trusting with their savings, Jason was disgusted. He agreed to cooperate and offer any information he had. He couldn't live with himself otherwise.

Yet he didn't expect his dad to be so calm about it.

Jason broke the silence. "You're not...angry?"

Marty sighed. "No. I'm not angry. Not with you."

Jason didn't know what to say. Did his dad understand the seriousness of the accusations against him? Did he understand that with the evidence the FBI had, he would probably be in jail for years?

Marty continued. "Things got out of control, you know, out of hand. When you were little, and you don't remember this, I was just like any other guy working at a bank. And when I saw that there were chances to make more money, I couldn't resist. I figured that we weren't hurting anybody – just a few suckers. I know it's hard to believe now, but everything I did, I did because I wanted a better life for you."

Jason gritted his teeth. Was his dad trying to guilt him now? That would be a nice touch on their already delicate father-son relationship.

Part of the reason that Jason offered to help his dad in the first place was because he wanted to spend more time with his dad. He was always working, and Jason wanted to learn from his father and follow in his footsteps. He wanted to make him proud.

Jason shook off the memories. He was an adult now, and he couldn't let his dad play mind games with him. "Is this some sort of a trick?"

"No, no," his father replied hurriedly. "Not this. This is real. I've had a lot of time to think about everything – how I ended up here. Why I ended up here. I lost sight of what's important. I have a lot to be ashamed of." He paused to rub his forehead. "Long story short, I'm not angry at you at all. I'm only angry at myself."

Jason took a deep breath and sat back. His dad could charm his way out of almost any situation, but it really didn't seem like he was spinning a tale this time. It seemed genuine.

Jason studied his face. For the first time in his life, his dad looked tired. He had bags under his eyes. His posture was slumped. He'd always been full of life, full of schemes. Today, he looked defeated.

How long had he been like this? For the past few years, Jason pulled away from anything that had to do with his dad, so he hadn't seen him at all. He spoke to him occasionally, for holidays and birthdays. After years of trying to convince him to stop with all the schemes, he finally gave up. Eventually, Jason knew that his only chance at a normal life was to leave it all behind, his dad included.

"Okay then," Jason finally replied. He had no choice but to believe him.

A waitress stopped at their table. Jason put in an order for coffee and his father ordered a soda. She asked if they were ready to order and they looked at each other, wide eyed, doing that universal shrug as if to say "I am if you are!"

The exchange seemed so normal, so casual, that Jason couldn't help but note the absurdity of it all. No one from the outside would be able to see the cracks in their relationship. They looked like two guys having a relaxing lunch, ordering a pair of bacon burgers.

"So much for your cholesterol," said Jason.

His dad shrugged. "I'll do better next time."

As they waited for their food to come out, Jason answered what felt like a barrage of questions about his work and his life. It was like his dad was trying to make up for the last few years when all he seemed to care about was making more money.

When he was twenty, he would have loved for his dad to be so interested in his life. But all of this interest was about thirteen years too late.

After twenty minutes, their burgers arrived, stacked high and crowded with french fries. Jason looked around the restaurant – it didn't seem like anyone was watching them. The FBI agents warned him to be careful, but perhaps he'd taken the paranoia a bit too far.

"Now Jason," Marty said, squirting some ketchup onto his plate. "I know that I'll probably be going away for a bit. Could be the rest of my life, who knows how many years I have left."

Jason cringed. It was one thing to think about his dad living out the rest of his years in prison, but it was an entirely different thing to hear it said out loud.

He cleared his throat. "Yeah. That's what I heard."

Marty dipped a french fry in ketchup. "And I know that you don't agree with how I did it, but like I said, everything I did was for you. I don't want you to have to wait until I croak to get the money I've saved."

Jason set his coffee cup down. "Dad – "

"Hear me out," he said, cutting him off. "There's nothing shady about this. I talked to my lawyer and I can leave you *everything*. You won't have to work as a carpenter anymore."

"I love being a carpenter," Jason replied. "And I don't need the money."

Marty shoved a clump of fries into his mouth, chewing as he spoke. "Jason, I don't think you realize how much money I'm talking." He dropped his voice. "Two *billion* dollars."

Jason crossed his arms. It was more than he expected, but it didn't sway him. The higher the number, the more people his dad scammed. "I won't accept any of it."

His dad gasped.

Jason shook his head. "I just can't, Dad."

Marty shook his head frantically, pointing to his throat.

"Are you choking?" Jason asked, hearing the panic in his own voice.

Marty's face turned red.

Jason didn't know what to do. He stood up, darting to his dad's side, trying to remember what the procedure was in a situation like this. His mind was totally blank. He stood there, mouth open, gaping at his father with no idea how to help him.

Out of nowhere, a cascade of long hair crossed in front of Jason's sight. The next thing he saw was a pair of arms wrapped around his father's chest, the hands folded into a fist that thrusted under his sternum.

"Alright big guy," the woman called out. She continued speaking between thrusts. "We are not – going to let – you choke!"

A soggy clump of french fries flew from Marty's mouth onto the floor. He gasped for air and the woman patted him on the back.

"See?" she said with a smile. "I told you I wouldn't let you choke."

Jason stood there, his mouth still hanging open. His mind was too slow to catch up with what happened. He still felt panicked, even though he could see that his dad was breathing – no, laughing.

"Dad, are you okay?"

"Yeah, yeah, I'm fine." He dabbed at his forehead with his napkin. "Just tried to shove too many fries in at once, I guess."

He laughed and the woman laughed with him. She even let out a little snort.

"I'm glad you're okay," she said. "Does anything hurt?"

"Not at all," Marty replied, patting his belly. "I've been saved by an angel."

"Oh yeah right," she said with a giggle.

"You know," Marty said without missing a beat, "I always hoped my son would find a *strong* woman!"

Jason stared at him, horrified. How was it that his dad maintained the ability to completely embarrass him after all of these years? Was it like riding a bicycle, a skill he'd never lose?

She handled the awkward comment with grace. "That was my workout for the day, so thank you."

She smiled and turned to leave.

Jason wanted to say something, but still couldn't think straight. He was stunned with what happened.

She really *was* strong. And he was surprised that she was able to get her arms around his dad's big belly. She was tall, maybe even as tall as his dad. For some reason, that was all that his brain could focus on.

He continued gaping as she disappeared through the front door. The moment to thank her passed. Jason sat down at the table and focused his eyes back on his dad.

"One fry at a time, okay?"

"Forget the fries," his dad said, mouth full. "This burger is delicious!"

Chapter 2

Alex rushed to her car. She was already running late before stopping into the diner to grab lunch, and then she saw that guy choking! She couldn't just leave him there. Luckily, it was an easy rescue. It only took a few Heimlich thrusts and the man was back to his burger. Alex stuffed the rest of her donut into her mouth as she started her car.

She got to clinic with just enough time to say hello to the front end staff, wash her hands, and check her schedule for the day. She was excited to see that her first patient was one of her favorites.

"Mrs. Higgins! It's so lovely to see you," Alex said as she walked into the room.

Mrs. Higgins flashed a little smile. "And it's always nice to see you Dr. Small."

"What brings you in today? Nothing wrong I hope?"

"Oh no, you know me. Tough as a bag of nails. A 90 year old bag of nails."

Alex laughed. "Yes, of course. But you know that you can always tell me if you're having any trouble."

Mrs. Higgins smiled. "I know, kiddo. That's why I keep coming to see you."

Alex completed a physical exam and reviewed all of Mrs. Higgins' most recent blood work. It was all wonderfully normal. Mrs. Higgins had nothing new to report, except for some pictures of her great-grandchildren.

Alex loved baby pictures. She oohed and gushed over their chubby cheeks.

Mrs. Higgins tucked the pictures back into her purse. "Dr. Small, you know that I worry about you."

"Me? Why?" she replied, though she knew what was coming.

"You can't be a day over 26, but you won't be young forever. Don't forget to find a nice man to start a family with."

Alex almost corrected her to say that she was 31, not 26, but she stopped herself when she realized that it would only make her situation seem worse.

"I'm working on it," she said with a wink.

Mrs. Higgins stood up and fetched a plastic container from her purse. "I made these this morning, just for you and the girls."

Chocolate chip cookies. Alex loved Mrs. Higgins' cookies, but it made her feel guilty that this sweet 90 year old woman was getting up early to bake for them.

"You're too good to us. You know that we all love your baking, but I don't want you to feel like you have to trouble yourself like that just to come in and see us."

Mrs. Higgins pulled her in for a hug. "Oh hush, an old lady likes to feel useful once in a while."

Alex escorted her to the front lobby, carrying the container with her. The rest of the staff spotted the cookies at once and demanded that she open them immediately. Alex obliged; she was happy that Mrs. Higgins could see how much her efforts were appreciated.

The rest of Alex's day flew by; she always liked coming up to this clinic. She was part of a group of doctors who traveled between a handful of the rural clinics in the area, and her schedule at this spot in particular was always packed.

After she finished medical school, she wanted to move back home to be close to her parents. She interviewed at several primary care offices in her hometown of Albany, New York, but none of them felt quite right.

The offices were fine, of course; the other doctors seemed nice and the staff was hardworking. Yet none of them had a mission that inspired her as much as the rural health clinic group – the doctors there traveled around to ensure that the people of upstate New York got the care they deserved.

It was a shame that there was such a shortage of doctors in the area. Her interview there felt like a dream come true and she accepted the job offer immediately. Alex was happy to contribute, even in her small way.

Since most of the clinics were north of Albany, she had to live a bit further from her parents, but she didn't mind. The scenery more than made up for it – it was an absolutely breathtaking part of the country.

She didn't have a chance to take a break that day until 5 PM when her last patient of the day was a no show. She was surprised; Mr. Willow had never missed an appointment before.

"Do you want me to give him a call?" asked Jean, one of Alex's favorite nurses.

"I would really appreciate it if you could," Alex said. "Tell him that if he's not feeling well, I can stop by on my way home and check on him."

"Okay, I'll let him know."

Alex wandered into the break room in search of something to eat. All she had eaten that day was half a bagel for breakfast and that donut for lunch. Her morning clinic in the next town over ran late, which led to a domino effect of lateness.

It was all for a good reason, though. Her last patient of the morning came in crying, devastated by the loss of her husband the previous month. Alex sat with her, holding her hand and listening to her. She tried to offer as much comfort as she could. Though she wished she could do more, the *least* she could do was share her time. Falling a bit behind schedule was a small price to pay.

The break room fridge had nothing but week-old pizza; Alex gave it a sniff and recoiled. As hungry as she was, it wasn't worth getting food poisoning.

She settled on pouring herself a mug of coffee. It was unfortunate that all of Mrs. Higgins' cookies were gone, because they would've been great with coffee. She wished she'd stashed one for herself earlier.

Oh well! There would always be next time. Mrs. Higgins insisted on bringing something every time she came.

Maybe by the next time they saw each other, Alex would be able to tell Mrs. Higgins that she was actually seeing someone. What would she say if she knew her real age? Or that she hadn't been on a date in years?

Alex knew that things wouldn't change on their own – she'd have to make an effort if she wanted a relationship. Or, for that matter, if she ever wanted to have the family she'd always imagined. There were a lot of excuses she'd made over the years as to why it wasn't the right time.

The biggest was that her job took up a lot of time. But she loved her job. It was always her dream to be a doctor, and it seemed like she worked her entire life to get to this point.

She had a boyfriend once – Brian. They met in college and dated for two years. He was a wonderful guy, and she thought for sure that someday they would get married and start a family.

But life doesn't always turn out the way that you expect. When Alex got into her dream medical school in North Carolina, she didn't hesitate to accept.

Alex didn't like to overthink things that felt right, and this definitely felt right. Brian gave her his full support, too, even though he had a job back in Syracuse that meant they'd have a nine hour drive between them.

She believed that she and Brian would be able to work it out. Their love was strong enough to survive the distance.

And maybe it was strong enough to survive the distance. But it wasn't strong enough to survive Brian's stressful job, Alex's constant studying, and Brian's mom being diagnosed with cancer.

After the first year, he told her that he just couldn't do it anymore.

She could have dropped out of medical school then and there, moved back up North, and married him. She knew, though, that if she did that, it was unlikely she would ever go back to school to finish her training.

It was one of the hardest decisions she ever had to make. She loved Brian with all of her heart. She wanted to be there for him. But when she thought about giving up her seat at school, she just couldn't do it. She couldn't abandon that chance to make her dream come true.

It broke her heart to say goodbye to him, but in the back of her mind, she always hoped that one day they would end up together again.

That didn't work out, of course. Alex pulled out her phone and navigated to Brian's Facebook page. She clicked on his profile picture – it was him, his wife, and their two beautiful children.

She stared at it for a moment, studying their smiles. She didn't feel bitter or angry. It's not like she didn't *want* Brian to be happy. He was a wonderful guy – he deserved to be happy.

In a selfish way, she felt sad for herself. It was sad that life made her choose between a great person, whom she loved with all of her heart, and her lifelong dream of being a doctor.

Mrs. Higgins was right, though. What was Alex waiting for? If 26 was pushing it for starting a family, 31 was practically ancient. If she wanted to have a husband and have little rugrats of her own, she needed to do something about it.

Alex stuck her phone back in her pocket. That was that. It was time to revive her love life. She wasn't sure exactly how she'd do it, but surely the first step was committing to change, right?

"Alex?" Jean popped her head into the break room.

"Hey Jean, what's up?"

"I called Mr. Willow. First he apologized for not calling us, said he overslept with a nap."

Alex smiled. "Oh, okay, I'm glad he's not sick."

Jean frowned. "He said he's been sleeping a lot lately, and that he's getting so tired because he can't catch his breath."

"Oh dear," Alex said with a sigh. "I wonder if his heart failure is flaring up. He might be carrying extra fluid that's making it harder to breath."

Jean shrugged. "Could be."

"Or maybe pneumonia again...he had it last year. He's still smoking so he's definitely at risk..."

"I tried to offer him some of the free nicotine patches," Jean replied. "He said he wasn't ready to quit yet."

Alex stood up. "Yeah, I remember. I appreciate that you're trying. One day he might be ready. Anyways – if you guys don't need anything from me, I think I'll stop over to his place and see what's going on."

"Sounds good, we're all set here."

"Alright Jean, thanks for all of your help today! See you guys next week!"

"Take care!"

Alex stopped by a computer to write down Mr. Willow's address before saying goodbye and getting into her car. Finding a husband would have to wait, at least for tonight. She told herself that maybe over the weekend she could join a dating website or something.

For now she was going to check on one of her notoriously stubborn patients and drive him to the emergency room, if need be.

Chapter 3

Jason and Marty finished lunch without any additional near-death experiences. His dad wanted to pick up the tab, but Jason was one step ahead of him and made sure to pay for it first.

He paid with cash to avoid leaving any traces of their meeting behind. He still felt wary that they may have been followed, so he told his dad that they shouldn't linger in the parking lot in case anyone was watching.

Marty dismissed the fear. "Don't worry about it, son. What could they even do to me now?"

"A lot," Jason replied. The FBI agents told him how aggressive his dad's enemies were. It seemed unwise not to be afraid.

Marty shrugged. "I guess. Well, you stay safe."

"You too." Jason struggled for something more to say. This wasn't at all how he expected this meeting to go. And now, he found himself quite sentimental in his last moments with his father as a free man.

"Hey, don't look so glum. I always knew this was coming. I'm surprised I've lasted so long."

Jason offered a pained smile. "That's one way to look at it."

His dad patted him on the shoulder. "Don't worry so much. The next time I see you, it'll be in court. I've got a new suit!"

What a thing to say. "Alright Dad."

"Take care."

Jason watched as his dad got into a flashy Jaguar. Definitely not the kind of car that Jason would've chosen for what was supposed to be a secret meeting, but it only further supported the fact that Jason had no control over what his dad did.

He sighed. Even if his dad deserved to go to jail, it made him feel sick to think about.

Jason walked over to his old beat up pickup truck. Though he couldn't shake the feeling of sadness around this meeting, he at least felt good that he was honest with his dad and met with him in person. He finally felt ready to tell the FBI that he was ready to go all in.

It took him forty minutes to get back to his small, dark hotel room because he took the long way to ensure he wasn't followed. It wasn't the nicest place, but he wanted to get away from home and get the chance to talk to his dad about what he was doing.

He'd only been there for about a week, though it felt like it'd been a lifetime since the FBI agents came to talk to him at his home in Virginia. They told him about his dad's trial, which he hadn't heard about, and asked if he had any information that would help the case against his dad.

He was too stunned to think clearly, so they gave him a night to think about it. The next day, his house was ransacked while he was at work. The windows were broken, closets and shelves were turned inside out, floorboards were ripped up and worst of all – they set his workshop on fire, along with all of his woodworking projects inside.

At first, when he walked into that scene, he thought there was some sort of a terrible accident. It took a few minutes for him to come to his senses and tell the FBI that he was targeted.

They told him that he had two options: he could agree to go into temporary protection while the U.S. Marshals determined if he was a candidate for the witness protection program, or he could take his chances with the criminals who destroyed his home.

He planned to choose the temporary protection and told the FBI agents everything he knew about his dad's "businesses." At first, he wasn't sure that anything he had to say would be worthwhile – years earlier, he'd documented the names and numbers that his dad told him, but he didn't know what any of it meant.

It wasn't until he mentioned that he still had copies of all the records that the agents' eyes lit up. They escorted him back to his house, got the computer, and told Jason that this collection of documents was the jackpot.

His father was involved in many different scams over the years and with that, he was deeply entangled with numerous shady business associates. Jason's records connected all of these associates, along with dates and even payment information. It was no wonder that the goons wanted to scare Jason into keeping his mouth shut.

Jason locked the door to the hotel room and pulled out the cell phone that the FBI agents gave him. The agents were his only contacts – it made him laugh a little at how absurd it all was. It was happening so quickly that he was having a hard time accepting that he actually was leaving his entire life behind.

Though when he was honest with himself, he knew that he didn't have much to show for his life. Sure, he would miss the people that he worked with and all of his friends.

But even that life was something he built after running away from his dad and his dad's problems. Jason spent his entire life running away. He was tired of it. As hard as it was to leave everything behind, he was ready to start over, one last time.

He dialed Agent Simmons.

"Agent Simmons, what's up?"

Jason smiled. When he first interacted with Agent Simmons, he thought it was odd that he answered the phone like that – but then he realized that he was in the FBI and he could do whatever he wanted. It all seemed impossibly cool to him.

"Hi, it's Jason Brash. I'm ready to come in."

"That's great news. Have you decided if you're going to enter witness protection?"

"Yes. If that offer is still available, I would like to take it."

"Alright Jason. We were hoping you'd say that. Hang tight, we'll be out to pick you up in an hour. Make sure to pack anything that you don't want to leave forever."

Jason looked around the empty room. He wouldn't have much to bring. "Alright, sounds good. Thank you."

The next hour dragged on. When Jason left his home in Virginia, he only brought what could fit in the back of his truck. He told himself that he was just going to visit his dad in Albany and explore his options, but deep down he knew that he would never return.

Most important to him were his tools and a photo album of his family – back when they were happy. He wondered if they would take that from him. Though he was just a baby in most of the pictures, his dad was easily recognizable, with his wild eyes and bad haircut.

He loved those pictures, though. His mom looked happy; it was before his dad's greed took over their lives. Jason's mom, Sandra, couldn't stand what her husband turned into. She hated the lies and the scams. She hated the never-quite-above-board business ideas. Most of all, she hated the feeling that the money didn't come from a good place, even if her husband was skilled at lying about how he got it.

Just a few years after the divorce, his mom passed away from cancer and he had to go back and live with his dad. She never spoke poorly of his dad, which was a civility he may not have deserved; in the end, it hurt Jason because he had no idea what kind of a person his father really was.

Jason pushed the memories aside and repacked a small suitcase of clothing. He set it next to his tools by the front door and then sat on the couch waiting for the FBI to arrive.

True to their word, they arrived almost exactly one hour after the phone call was made. Jason opened the door and welcomed them inside.

"Hey Jason, good to see you," Agent Simmons said, vigorously shaking his hand.

"Good to see you too."

Agent Simmons was the first person who contacted him in Virginia, and he threw Jason because he was so unlike what he thought an FBI agent would be. He always imagined that agents were serious, no-nonsense, dark sunglass wearing forces of the law. He got that from the movies mostly, and maybe some were like that.

But Agent Simmons was more like a friendly dad. He had salt-and-pepper hair, twinkling blue eyes, and always sported a wide smile. He was just about Jason's dad's age, which made Jason wonder what his life would have been like if his father chose a life of law enforcement instead of a life of financial crime.

A woman he'd never seen before stepped forward. "Hi Jason, I'm U.S. Marshal Madeline Perez."

"Nice to meet you."

"It looks like you're ready to go."

"I am," he replied. "I hope that this isn't too much to bring."

Simmons laughed. "No, not at all. Usually we have to talk people out of bringing several carloads of stuff. This is no problem."

Perez smiled. "You should see what some of the mobster housewives try to bring with them."

Jason laughed. "I can't imagine."

She made a motion to pick up his suitcase.

"Please," he said, intercepting her. "I can carry it. Don't trouble yourself."

She gave him a stern look, but let him pick up the tools and his bag.

It wasn't that he thought she couldn't handle carrying his stuff – she was clearly a tough woman. It just seemed impolite. She stood at what could be no more than 5'3", yet she commanded the room. Unlike Agent Simmons, she was not constantly smiling. Jason figured that as a woman in her position, she probably didn't have the luxury of being overly friendly.

Jason liked her immediately; she reminded him of his mother. She was also a no-nonsense sort of woman.

They walked out to a black SUV and Jason loaded his stuff in the back.

"I guess I'll have to leave my truck behind?"

Simmons nodded. "Yeah, but don't worry. Where you're going, I bet they'll have a nice truck for you."

"Really?" For some reason, this cheered him a bit.

"We've got you covered," said Perez with a smile.

They drove along for about half an hour before they reached their destination.

"This is a secure location where you will spend the night before we send you to your new home," said Perez.

"You know," commented Simmons, "I half expected you to stand us up."

Jason shot him a puzzled look. "Why?"

Though his father was a dishonest man, Jason certainly was not. He felt a bit of shame burn in his chest – of course people would assume that he was just like his father.

"Well," he said with a sigh, "to start, we don't have much to offer you. Most of the people that go into witness protection are guilty of crimes themselves. But you haven't done anything wrong. You could just keep living your life the way that it was."

"That's not entirely true," Jason said as he stepped into the building. "I've felt guilty for long enough. I felt like this was the least I could do to bring justice for some of the people that my dad scammed over the years."

Simmons continued. "Yeah, well, when you met with him today, we thought you might be tipping him off."

Jason shook his head. "No. I needed him to know what I was doing, though."

Perez smiled. "We know. We heard it all."

Jason took a step back. "So I was followed? I knew it."

Simmons shook his head. "No, we didn't follow you. But some of your father's associates knew that you were meeting. Before you got there, they bugged the restaurant. And we have them tapped, so we got to listen in, too."

"Seriously?" Jason felt like the wind was knocked out of him. "Are you saying that my dad set me up?"

"No," Simmons said quickly. "It doesn't appear that your dad was involved at all. I think he was quite unaware. They're not happy with him, though. And they're really not happy with you."

They walked down a long hallway and invited Jason into a well lit room. He took a seat.

"Yeah, I know. I'm a big problem for them."

"We appreciate what you're doing," Perez said.

Simmons closed the door. "We do. Your testimony helps connect a lot of dots. I'm glad that you came in when you did, because we've been hearing a lot of chatter that they want to intimidate you and prevent you from testifying."

Jason frowned. "And have they found anything to use against me? They already destroyed my home."

Agent Simmons shook his head. "No. Luckily not. You have no family, no children, and no discernible significant other."

Jason knew that Simmons didn't mean to sound so harsh, but wow – when he put it like that, Jason sounded like a loser.

Perez frowned. "Well there was one thing. They're investigating the woman that you met at the diner."

"What woman?" asked Jason, scrunching his brows.

"The audio cut out a bit, but it sounded like she saved your dad from choking."

How could he forget? She swept in and out like nothing happened. The woman who seemed larger than life. Her hair was impossibly long and her arms were impossibly strong. Strong enough to wrap around his dad's big belly and force a bunch of french fries out of his wind pipe.

"But I don't know her," he protested.

Perez shot Simmons a worried look.

"Is she in some sort of trouble?" Jason asked, studying their faces.

Simmons waved a hand. "I'm sure that once they realize that you don't know her, no harm will come to her."

"What do you mean? Are they looking for her?"

Perez nodded. "It seems like they are. Your dad made a comment about you finding a 'strong woman?' "

Jason shook his head. "He was just being weird. I don't know her."

"They haven't found her yet," said Perez. "They have a very poor quality picture of what she looks like that they stole from a hacked security camera nearby."

"We hacked in and got the same picture," Agent Simmons interjected. "It's pretty blurry. They may never find her."

Jason felt his stomach sink. It was one thing to send his father to jail, and another thing to put himself in harm's way. But he couldn't live with himself if his actions put a stranger – no, a good Samaritan – in danger.

"Do you guys know who she is?"

"We do," Perez said with pursed lips.

"Then it's only a matter of time before they find her, too." Jason stood up from his chair. "She deserves to know that they're looking for her, and she deserves to know that she's in danger."

Simmons crossed his arms. He was not smiling anymore. "That may be difficult. We can't offer her protection. She's not involved in the case."

Jason crossed his arms. "What if I say she is my girlfriend? Then what?"

For a moment, they all looked at each other, absorbing the silence.

"Are you making her protection a condition of your testimony?" asked Perez carefully.

Jason almost replied no at first – he hated making a fuss. But then he realized that she was giving him a way to protect the mystery woman.

"Yes. I am. I will not testify unless this woman is also under your protection."

Agent Simmons clapped his hands together. "Alright then! Looks like we have some work to do."

Chapter 4

Checking on Mr. Willow didn't take long. Luckily, he didn't need to go to the hospital. She was glad that she went to see him, though, because the dose of the water pill for his heart failure definitely needed to be increased.

After some debate, Alex got him to promise that he would weigh himself daily and call the clinic if he had more than a three pound weight gain.

Patients loved it when she popped in. And Alex loved being able to do that for them. It was something she'd never be able to do if she were at a bigger practice.

She got home late that night, but since it was Friday, she knew she could sleep in late the next morning.

To her surprise, she was awoken by a knock at the door around seven in the morning.

"Who on earth could that be?" she said as she pulled on a robe. Peering through the peephole, she saw a woman with her hair pulled back in a tight ponytail. Behind her stood a serious looking man in a suit.

Alex opened the door. "Hi, how can I help you?"

The woman spoke first. "Are you Dr. Alexandra Small?"

"Yes?"

The woman offered her hand. "Dr. Small, my name is Madeline Perez. I am a Deputy U.S Marshal and this is Agent Darkwood with the FBI."

The man nodded in acknowledgment. They both pulled out their badges.

"Would it be alright if we came in to speak to you for a moment?"

Was this some sort of strange dream?

"Sure," Alex said, a bit self conscious now about the sweatpants and robe that she wore to answer the door. "Come on in."

She led them into the living room and offered them a seat on the couch.

"Would you like any coffee or tea?"

"No, thank you," Perez replied.

Alex took a seat across from them. "Has there been...some sort trouble?"

Perez shook her head. "*You* are not in any trouble, Dr. Small. Not with us."

"Oh good!" Alex laughed. She'd never broken a law in her life, but that didn't stop her mind from jumping to conclusions that perhaps she'd unknowingly done something extremely illegal. Did government agents show up at your door if you didn't fully stop at a stop sign? That seemed extreme.

Perez continued. "But we do think that you may be in some danger."

"Oh." Alex leaned forward. "What do you mean?"

Perez pulled out a folder and slid it forward. Opening the cover, Alex discovered a grainy picture of herself from what looked like security footage.

"Dr. Small, do you remember going to Lou's Diner yesterday?"

"Yeah, of course. I got a donut for lunch."

"Do you remember anything unusual about your visit?"

She thought for a moment. Had she forgotten to pay for the donut and accidentally stolen it?

"I don't think so?" she finally responded. "The donut was really good. I don't normally get jelly filled, but that was all they had and I'm glad I went for it."

Agent Darkwood looked at her like she'd just said the dumbest thing on earth. She felt her cheeks flush a little, but it *was* unusual for her to get a jelly filled donut!

Perez moved Alex's picture to the side; beneath it was a mug shot of a guy. "Do you recognize this man?"

Alex leaned in to study the photograph. "I can't say that I do."

Perez continued. "This is Marty Brash. He is currently awaiting trial for decades of insider trading, running a boiler room and scamming thousands of people out of their savings."

"What's a boiler room? Like to heat a building?"

Perez smiled. "No. It's a call center where salesmen sell bad investments to people."

"Oh," she nodded as if she understood. Had her retirement account been hacked? She didn't even have much money in there.

Perez continued. "Do you recall performing the Heimlich maneuver yesterday?"

"Oh! Yes, I do." She nodded enthusiastically. "A guy choked on a bunch of french fries. Was it this Marty guy?"

"It was," Perez replied. "And by saving his life, you unfortunately may have become a target of some of his associates."

"Target for what?"

Darkwood chimed in. "Dr. Small – "

She interrupted him. "Please, call me Alex."

He smiled. "Alex. I work in white collar and financial crime. It's not as common for white collar criminals to use violence to intimidate witnesses, but it certainly does happen. Marty is currently await-ing trial, and to make a long story short, there is a lot of information that his former partners do not want getting out."

"Oh my," Alex said.

"They're circulating this photograph of you to try to discover your identity, because they think you may be a friend of his. Well – a friend of his son's."

Alex shook her head in disbelief. "Why? I don't know Marty. I just walked by and saw a guy choking."

Darkwood continued. "And they may realize that you don't know him once they talk to you. But they are getting very desperate, and I'm not sure what they might do if they found you."

Alex sat back and crossed her arms over her chest. "I can't believe this is real."

"Unfortunately, it is," Perez said with a sigh. "We were lucky enough to find you before they did. And we would like to offer you a place in our witness security program, WITSEC."

"Is that like witness protection? I thought that was only in the movies!"

Perez laughed. "No, it's real. And it's a very successful program for keeping people safe."

Alex looked around the room, wondering if she was going to wake up any minute. "I can't just leave my life behind. I can't leave my patients behind."

"Your life is in danger," Darkwood said flatly. "This is the only protection that we can offer you."

That seemed drastic. Couldn't she just meet up with these guys and tell them she had nothing to do with this criminal? Surely they would all have a good laugh about it.

Perez broke the silence. "I understand that this is a lot to take in. But unlike many of the people who go into the program, your stay would likely be short-term. Just until our witness completes his testimony at trial. Possibly six weeks or so."

"Oh, so it wouldn't be the rest of my life?"

"No," responded Perez.

"That's better than forever, I guess."

Alex stared at them. How could she even be sure they were who they said they were? They flashed their badges, but she didn't know what she was looking for. Was it possible that this was some sort of elaborate prank? Or that they were trying to kidnap her?

Darkwood stood up. "We're not safe here. We can take you to a safe location and discuss this further."

A safe location? That definitely sounded like something that a kidnapper would say.

Perez must have sensed her apprehension. She pulled out another folder. "Here is all of the information that the FBI was able to acquire in the last 12 hours. If the criminals are able to get ahold of your name, then they will have all of this as well."

Alex opened the folder. There were pictures of her and her parents; driver's licenses; school records – everything. There was even a picture of her parents' house and the license plates to their cars!

"You guys realize how crazy this all is, right?" Alex said.

Darkwood was about to answer but Perez cut him off. "We do. But we are here to offer you some options. How about you put together a travel bag and we get to somewhere safe so we can talk more?"

It didn't seem like she had much of an option. Whether they actually were special agents or kidnappers, they didn't appear flexible about her next move. At least Marshal Perez seemed trustworthy. Agent Darkwood probably was too, but he was a bit more pushy than Alex liked.

"Alright, give me a few minutes," she said.

Alex had no idea what was appropriate to pack for leaving her life behind, so she ended up with a jumbled suitcase stuffed with a few favorite sweaters, a swimsuit (because what if she got to go somewhere with a beach?), and things she randomly grabbed from her closet. She took the chance to change out of her sweatpants and into jeans as well.

She went back into the living room and without a word, they escorted her out of the front door and into a black SUV. Once they were in the car, Marshal Perez made some official sounding phone calls that made Alex feel better. As crazy as it all was, it did at least seem like they were real government agents.

They arrived at an unassuming building. Once inside, Alex was impressed to see an active room of ringing phones and a bunch of people buzzing around. At that point, she was fully convinced that this was the real FBI. Or U.S. Marshals. Or whatever. It was comforting how legitimate it seemed.

What was not comforting was the fact that she actually *was* in some serious danger.

Perez took her to a small room and offered her a bagel and some coffee. Alex didn't feel hungry, but she accepted the coffee since it might help her feel a little sharper for what was to come.

Over the next hour, Perez explained in detail what the witness security program would do for her. She'd be given an entirely new identity with a new driver's license, passport, and a fake job. All of her lodging and accommodations would be paid for, and her parents would be under 24 hour surveillance to ensure they were not targeted, too.

"As I said before, this is a bit of an unusual case because you won't require witness protection for the rest of your life. We are confident that once the trial is completed, they will give up."

"What if they don't?"

"Let's not think that way," Perez said gently. "So really, you can think of this as an all inclusive vacation."

Alex laughed. "I like your attitude. And I've never been on an all inclusive vacation before, so this may be really nice."

Perez pulled back. "Really?"

Alex shrugged. "Well, no."

Her parents didn't have much money growing up, but they did make the occasional camping trip or visit to the lake. Then she went to college and medical school and residency. Once she was a doctor... well, the thought crossed her mind that she could take a fancy vacation or a cruise or something, but she never got around to it.

She loved her job, and though she sometimes felt the urge to get away and recharge, it seemed wasteful to spend money on a trip for herself when she still had so much debt from medical school. She preferred to stay home or visit a friend when she had some time off.

Perez smiled. "Well then, I'd say that you're long overdue."

"I guess so." Alex took a sip of coffee. "The thing that bothers me most, though, is that my parents won't know where I'm going and they'll be really worried. And my patients rely on me. I can't disappear like this."

Perez nodded. "I thought of that, and we may be able to invent a cover story for you since it's such a short period of time. Plus, I believe that a sudden disappearance would most likely trigger a missing person search by your parents, which would not help our situation. I noticed in your file that you've done some mission trips to South America and Africa?"

"Yes," Alex said. "Medical mission trips."

"I'm thinking that we can tell a select few – your parents and your colleagues – that you've been pulled into a high priority, and dangerous, medical mission trip."

"Hm – do you think anyone would buy that?"

"We'll make it look pretty convincing," said Perez. "Do you trust their discretion? If you tell them that they need to keep your location secret, even though they won't really know where you are, do you think they can do that?"

"Absolutely," Alex replied. "If I tell them that I could be in danger if my location is released, I'm sure that they will happily cover for me. They'll say that I took a vacation."

"Okay, good. We can work with that."

"Oh! I have one more request," Alex said. "Would I be able to tell this story to one of my coworkers? She had a baby a few months ago and has been working limited hours, but if I asked her to cover my patients for me, I know that she would. And I wouldn't feel like I was abandoning them."

"That seems fine, I'll run it by my boss," Perez said.

Alex leaned back in her chair. It felt like a weight came off of her chest. "Thank you."

"We'll get to work on your backstory right now. I'll show you to a room where you can relax before making some calls about your 'mission trip,' okay?"

Alex stood up excitedly. "Okay, I guess we're doing this!"

"Don't worry," said Perez as she led Alex down the hall. "You're in good hands."

The waiting room was surprisingly comfortable – it was basically a hotel room. Alex stretched out on the bed and grabbed the TV remote. Part of her was scared by the fact that she was on some sort of a hit list for a bunch of criminals. Yet the other, and possibly larger, part of her was excited.

Her mother always teased her for being exceedingly positive and finding the good in every situation. But this was like a movie come to life! She was involved in a top secret program. She was getting a new identity. And as long as neither she nor her family were in any danger, she really could convince herself that it was a free, all inclusive vacation.

Maybe they would send her to a tropical island? That would be cool. Or maybe she would get to hide out in a city – Paris or Rome! Alex flicked through the channels, her mind too busy to focus on watching anything.

She knew that she should probably feel more afraid, but she trusted the U.S. Marshals. Also, the timing seemed so perfect. Just yesterday, she decided that she needed to change her life. What an awesome jump to her new life this would be!

After about an hour, an agent knocked on her door to escort her to another room for a makeover. A young looking woman with dyed pink hair introduced herself.

"I'm Katy, and my job is to make sure that you're unrecognizable when you leave here."

That seemed a bit ominous. "Hi Katy, I'm Alex."

Katy looked her up and down. "Wow – how tall are you?"

"Five eleven," Alex said as she took a seat. She got a lot of questions about her height. It didn't help that her last name was "Small." It made the jokes too easy.

"Do you play basketball?" Katy asked as she undid Alex's ponytail.

People were always asking her about basketball or volleyball. "No, no basketball. I'm not really athletic."

"Hm..." Katy said, tapping her chin.

"What?" asked Alex.

"You're not going to like this, but we definitely need to cut this long hair of yours."

Somehow this seemed worse to Alex than having to leave her life behind for a few weeks. "But I've always had long hair!"

Katy looked down at her knowingly. "Exactly. Way too recognizable. Don't worry – it'll grow back. And I have some great ideas about what we can do."

Alex bit her lip. "How short are you going to go?"

"Don't worry about it," Katy said. "You're going to love it, or you can tell them to fire me."

"I would never do that," Alex said quickly.

Katy laughed. "Great. Then let me work my magic."

After two hours of washing, foiling, cutting and drying, Katy finally let Alex look in the mirror again. She was stunned by what she saw. Her hair was cut just above her shoulder, streaked with delicate blonde highlights. There were some shorter pieces around her face and it looked so much fluffier than it did before.

"What do you think?" Katy said anxiously.

"It looks...amazing!" Alex said. "I can't believe...I mean, you did such a great job!"

"Good! I told you not to worry. With your hair texture, cutting it shorter gives it more body. And these highlights really soften your natural color."

"They really do!" Alex mentally scolded herself for not having done this sooner. It looked great!

"Oh, the agents got your eyeglass prescription and ordered you some contact lenses."

Alex frowned. "But I love my glasses."

"Hand 'em over," Katy said, hand outstretched. "Do you know how to put contacts in?"

Alex sighed, removing her glasses. "Yes, I just don't like contacts. I haven't worn any for years"

"These are the same kind I use, you'll like them. They're new. They don't dry your eyes out as much."

Alex looked at the box of contacts. Well, everything about this trip couldn't be perfect. She'd make do.

Next, she met with Marshal Perez again. She provided her with documentation and a full history for the fake medical trip that she would tell everyone she was taking. The fake organization for the trip had a website, a working phone number, plus pictures and tons of information. Alex was really impressed with what they managed to build in such a short time.

Perez sat with her as she called a handful of people to let them know that she was leaving immediately. It all went a lot better than she expected. Though she felt guilty lying to her parents, she knew that she could tell the truth once it was all over. It wasn't like she had a choice – if she refused the help of WITSEC, she would be on her own. That didn't seem like a smart choice. She knew that once her parents heard the full story, they would agree with what she chose.

By the end of it all, she felt exhausted. Perez told her to get some rest, because next she needed to memorize her new identity and prepare to fly out in the morning.

Perez had one last piece of advice before she made her exit. "Remember – no harm has ever come to anyone in the witness protection program who followed our rules. But if you leave your designated area or contact anyone from your previous life, we won't be able to protect you. Do you understand?"

Alex nodded. "Of course! Why on earth would I want to break the rules?"

With that, she went back to get some sleep and prepare for the next steps of her journey.

Chapter 5

"Mr. Aiken?"

Jason spun around. He was still getting used to being "Mitchell Aiken." He had to start thinking of himself as Mitch so he wouldn't make any mistakes once he got to his new witness protection location in Cody, Wyoming.

Initially, the plan was that he would drive into Cody in his new pickup truck and move into a rental house. However, the U.S. Marshals wanted him to wait until they could bring both him and his dad's Heimlich maneuver savior into town.

He thought that he'd have to wait for at least a week, but the Marshals worked astonishingly fast. They located her and then made her a new identity in a day.

Apparently, she was given two choices: join him in Cody, which was already a prepared and secure site, or wait out the next six weeks in the holding facility. The Marshals explained to her that they wouldn't have another site approved and prepared for her quickly enough otherwise.

She picked Cody. Mitch hoped she'd like it.

"Hey, good to see you again," Mitch said, once he realized he was being addressed. It was funny to see Agent Simmons in anything but his usual suit – now he *really* just looked like a happy dad, wearing faded jeans and a t-shirt.

"Good to see you too. I'd like you to meet Deputy U.S. Marshal Turner. This is where I take my leave."

Mitch shook Marshal Turner's hand. He too was dressed casually. Jason felt disappointed that he wouldn't get to spend more time with Simmons.

"Nice to meet you."

Agent Simmons saw the confusion on Mitch's face. "Only the U.S. Marshals will know where you're hiding. It's for your own protection – but I'll see you in a few weeks at trial."

Mitch nodded. "Well – thank you for everything."

Turner shifted towards the door. "Ready to head out?"

"Sure."

Mitch felt nervous. He wondered if this woman who saved his dad would be angry with him. Of course she would be – who wouldn't be angry about being ripped away from their home?

Once they got into the car, they could speak more freely.

"You guys work fast," Mitch said.

Turner smiled. "We do what we can. So about your dad's savior. She – "

"Wait," Mitch interrupted. "I don't think that I should know anything about her real life, right? In case I mess up and blow her cover?"

Turner shrugged. "Normally I'd tell you a bit about her, but if you're worried, that's alright. You should know that she'll be going by 'Kayla Smith.' We explained the rules of the program to her. Our plan is that she will only need a few weeks of protection, so her identity doesn't need to last as long as yours does. She is very anxious to get back to work."

Mitch felt the guilt creeping in about bringing this woman into his mess. "Does she have a family? Is she leaving children behind?"

"No. No husband, no kids. If she did, we would take them in as well. So that makes it easier."

"Oh, okay." Mitch sat for a moment. He debated if he should ask any more questions – surely Turner wouldn't tell him more than he was supposed to know. "What does she do for a living?"

"She's a doctor. Family medicine, I think."

"Ah," Mitch replied, rubbing the back of his neck. "I guess that explains why she was able to do the Heimlich without even thinking."

Turner laughed. "It does, doesn't it?"

Mitch didn't know what else to say. It was good that the woman – er, Kayla – decided to accept the protection of the Marshals. Even though he felt bad that her good deed landed her in harm's way, he was glad that they were able and willing to bring her into witness protection. After a few weeks of inconvenience, she could go back to her normal life like nothing ever happened.

Turner spent the car ride explaining what would be expected of both of them.

"We decided that it would be safest to keep you both around Cody. We've mapped out the location and know that neither of you have any ties to the area. The risk of being recognized is low. She'll be staying at a nearby ranch as a guest under the guise of writing an article about tourism. Her cover is that she's a journalist."

"Makes sense."

That seemed like a decent cover job, especially compared to what he ended up with: insurance salesman.

It wasn't as easy as pretending to be a salesman – he actually had to learn about insurance and try to make a living that way. He wasn't allowed to work as a carpenter anymore. Even if he wanted to, all of his credentials were under his old name – the name that he can never go back to. In his new life, Mitch Aiken was an insurance salesmen.

Turner continued. "We would like the two of you to meet at least twice a week. Don't make it suspicious, obviously. You will need to make it look like you have formed a casual friendship. That way, you can both discuss any unusual activity or suspicious people that try to contact you."

"Should we expect that someone will try to make contact with us?" asked Mitch.

Turner shook his head. "I don't expect it, no. We'll be on the lookout as well, of course. But it's helpful that both of you remain alert."

"Yeah, agreed," Mitch replied.

"You can contact us at anytime, just like we discussed. And if you feel that you're in danger and you cannot get a message to us safely, we will send agents to help you."

"Thank you."

Mitch set a reminder in his phone to send the Marshals a regular signal that all was well. If he missed it, they would come to the rescue.

The thought of being in danger wasn't what worried him. What made him most uneasy was that there were so many resources dedicated to protecting him. He couldn't help but feel like it was a waste – not just because he didn't think anyone would find him, but also because the U.S. Marshals were so talented that he couldn't believe they had to waste their time monitoring his safety.

He expressed these thoughts to Agent Simmons and Marshal Perez when they first approached him. They assured him that the government was more than happy to offer him protection in exchange for his testimony. From their perspective, it was extremely rare for any white collar criminal to get jail time – let alone several of them at once.

"Rob a bank? You might get away with 10, or maybe 15 thousand dollars," Marshal Perez told him. "If you get caught, you could spend the next 40 years of your life in prison. But these scam artists – what we call white-collar criminals – these guys steal millions, sometimes billions of dollars. They really hurt people. And most of them? They don't even get a fine, let alone any jail time."

Agent Simmons added, "This is one of the biggest cases that we've handled in the last 10 years. I'm happy to work day and night if that means justice for these crimes."

Mitch pulled himself out of his thoughts and tried to make conversation for the rest of the drive. They mostly chatted about Cody – Mitch couldn't wait to get there. When the Marshals offered him a spot in WITSEC, they first asked him where he'd like to go. He named a handful of places, and once he was done, they told him that he couldn't go to any of the places that he just said. Their reasoning was that if he wanted to go there, he likely had some connection to the place that could compromise him.

Fair enough. They then told him they'd move him out West. He was glad that he didn't think of naming anything there – there was something so freeing about moving out West.

He'd never technically been west of Cincinnati before, but he always suspected that it would suit him. So far he'd only seen bits and pieces while flying and going to and from the hotel – everything was bigger and more beautiful than he even imagined.

The only thing left to do was to meet Kayla before heading into town. Hopefully she wouldn't be too much of a know it all since she was a doctor. Mitch hoped that she understood the seriousness of being in hiding. If she blew her own cover, it would leave him vulnerable as well.

Marshal Turner and Mitch arrived at the restaurant at 7:30 that evening. It was relatively empty, and Mitch was glad that they still had the Marshals with them to ensure that there was no suspicious activity before they headed to their final destination.

Mitch spotted Marshal Perez first – she looked very unlike herself in blue jeans and an interesting shirt with a large picture of a horse on it.

"Nice horse, Perez," Turner said as they sat down.

Perez stared at him with narrowed eyes. "Thanks, the wardrobe girls really got a kick out of this one."

Mitch said a quiet hello and stole a quick glance at Kayla – she looked different than he remembered. For some reason, he thought she had really long hair. She stood up to shake his hand; here his memory served him well. He remembered thinking that she was unusually tall. He could now see that she was almost as tall as he was.

"Nice to meet you," she said. "My name is – Kayla Smith."

"Hi," he replied. "I'm Mitch. Mitch Aiken."

"Wait," she dropped her voice, "is that what I'm supposed to call you?"

Was this some sort of joke? "Yes."

Turner laughed. "That's a good one, Kayla."

Mitch sat down without saying anything else. It didn't seem like a good time to crack jokes.

The waitress made her way to their table. "Hi there, my name is Alex and I'll be taking care of you tonight."

Kayla gasped. "That's my name too!"

"Get out!" the waitress said with a wide smile.

No really, Mitch thought. Kayla should "get out" of the restaurant after blowing her cover with *literally* the first person she met.

"Excuse me," Mitch said as he stood and walked to the front door. Marshal Turner hurriedly followed him.

Once they were outside, Turner said, "Come on Mitch, don't let one little slip up bother you."

"One little slip up?" He shook his head in disbelief. "It's literally the *first* thing you're not supposed to mess up."

Turner shrugged. "What can I tell you? There's an adjustment. It's not a big deal. That's part of the reason why we didn't just drop both of you off in town on day one."

"Maybe she needs a few days to learn the basics."

"Nah, she's a smart girl. She'll figure it out."

"If she's not smart enough to remember her name, how smart can she be?"

Mitch heard the sound of the restaurant door closing behind him. He turned around to see Kayla standing there, staring at him.

Chapter 6

"Do you boys mind coming back inside? I don't want to keep Alex waiting." Kayla smiled before turning around and walking back into the restaurant.

It was weird referring to the waitress with her real name while thinking of herself as "Kayla." Perez told her it would take some getting used to.

Sure, she shouldn't have told the waitress that her name was Alex too. But it was an honest mistake, and it didn't give Mitch the right to call her stupid. *He* was the stupid one! He probably got caught committing some dumb crime and now they both had to pretend to be new people.

They followed her into the restaurant and took their seats. Kayla was determined to act perfectly pleasant to Mitch, even though she now knew he was a jerk in addition to being a criminal.

Alex (the waitress) came back and got their orders after a few minutes. Since they were in public, they couldn't talk about anything related to the witness protection program or to their real identities.

Instead, Marshal Turner led much of the conversation discussing the history of the nearby national parks. Kayla was fascinated. She always wanted to visit the national parks, but prior to this, it seemed like she was destined to only see them in pictures. This was going to be incredible.

The only annoying thing, she now realized, was that she'd need to check in and meet with Mitch two to three times a week. When she first heard that she would have to do this, Kayla didn't think it was a big deal. But now she was dreading it. She'd have to make sure that she didn't say anything silly in front of Mitch and prove him right.

They ate quickly and Turner paid the bill.

"Well fellas," Perez said as she stood from the table, "safe travels."

"Hope to see you again soon," Kayla added with a smile.

"Yes, definitely," Mitch said a little too quickly.

He seemed uncomfortable. Good! He should be. Kayla made a mental note to be sure not to see him more than necessary.

When they got to the parking lot, Perez handed Kayla a set of car keys. "Here's your new rental."

"This is so exciting," said Kayla. "What kind of car is it again?"

"Nothing fancy," replied Perez. "Just a little Toyota. It doesn't look like much, but it's decked out with gear so you can contact us anytime. Oh, and the glass is bulletproof."

"Of course," Kayla said with a smile. She couldn't believe how casually Perez added that – oh, just a partially bulletproof Toyota. No big deal.

Kayla spotted it quickly; it was the cleanest car in the parking lot. She hopped into the driver's seat and made herself comfortable. She had to push the car seat all the way back to fit her legs in, but it worked.

She turned the key and got started. Perez followed her out of the parking lot; the plan was that she'd supervise her to make sure she got to the ranch safely, and after that, she'd be on her own.

Kayla found the drive enjoyable, but it was too dark to really admire the landscape. Also, she felt like she should focus on the road – she didn't know the rules around crashing a car that the government loaned her, but she couldn't imagine that they would be very pleased if it needed any repairs.

She arrived at the New Morning Ranch just after nine that night. The staff knew that she'd be arriving late, but she still felt bad for whoever had to wait up for her. She rushed into the main lodge, apologizing profusely.

"Don't you worry one bit," said the young woman standing behind the counter. "I don't mind at all and I'm happy that you made it safely. Welcome to the New Morning Ranch!"

"Thank you so much, I'm excited to be here."

"You're Kayla, right?"

She nodded.

"Nice to meet you Kayla, I'm Isabelle Conner. My dad and I run this ranch."

Kayla looked around admiringly. It was a truly stunning lodge. "It's very nice to meet you Isabelle. And the ranch is gorgeous."

"Thank you kindly! If you follow me, I can show you to your cabin."

Isabelle led her through the back doors of the lodge, down a winding path, and to a cabin nestled beneath a mammoth tree.

The cabin took her breath away when she first saw it – it looked so magical under the moonlight. There was a covered porch with rocking chairs in the front and warm lights poured from the windows. The only sounds around them were some crickets in the distance. She paused for a moment and took a deep breath, taking it all in, before following Isabelle inside.

"This looks even more amazing than the pictures online!" said Kayla.

A smile spread across Isabelle's face. "Thank you, that means a lot. If you have some time, I can go over some of the activities that we have here at the ranch."

"No, please," said Kayla. "I feel bad enough that you had to wait up for me. How about I catch you tomorrow morning? We can talk then."

Isabelle nodded. "Sure, that works too. Breakfast is served every day in the main lodge between 6 and 10 AM."

"I'll see you there," said Kayla.

She waited until Isabelle left to jump up and squeal. The cabin was gorgeous. There was a large wood burning fireplace, some cozy looking lounge chairs, and a snug little kitchen. She popped her head into the bedroom and saw that it had the same cozy feel as the rest of the cabin.

As excited as she was about being there, she was worn out from her travels. After taking a few pictures of the cabin with her new U.S. Marshal-issued cell phone, Kayla got ready for bed and slipped under the covers.

The next morning, she woke promptly at six. She still needed to get used to the time change. Even though she knew that she was just in a different time zone, it felt like she got back two hours of her life, like a little second chance. When she went back East, she'd have to return those two hours, but she planned to use them wisely now.

Kayla showered that morning and got dressed in one of the cute outfits that the wardrobe girls packed for her. She didn't have a chance to pack much when she left her apartment. Plus, she didn't know where she was going, so it was nice that the wardrobe girls gave her a bunch of clothing appropriate for a Wild West vacation.

She made her way to the main lodge, excited to see that it was alive with families chatting, laughing, and eating. She grabbed a plate and helped herself before taking a seat at a table.

It wasn't long before Isabelle found her. "Good morning Ms. Smith, nice to see you up so early!"

"Oh please," she replied. "Call me – Kayla."

Ha! Take that Mitch. It only took one day and she was getting her name right and everything.

"I hope that breakfast is to your liking?"

Kayla replied with a mouth full of food. "Oh, it's wonderful! I have a bad feeling that I'll gain a lot of weight during this trip."

Isabelle beamed. "It's only time to end your vacation once you can't button your pants anymore."

"Is that time to end the vacation or time to buy new pants?" joked Kayla.

Isabelle laughed, taking a seat at the table. "Daddy said that you're staying a while because you're writing an article?"

"Yes," replied Kayla, trying to chew through a big bite of biscuit while setting her mind to lie convincingly. "But don't worry, I only write nice things. Basically it's to convince people to take a vacation to Wyoming."

A look of relief washed over Isabelle's face. "Well that's good to hear, I'll admit that I was a bit...nervous."

"Please don't be!" Kayla silently cursed her cover story – she didn't mean to scare these poor people! She wasn't even a real journalist. "And besides, it's not like I'm all that popular anyway. I write for a little online paper."

"Oh, neat! Well – do you wanna hear about some of our activities now?"

It seemed like her lie passed. "Sure!"

Isabelle jumped up. "Give me a second and I'll grab some of our brochures."

Kayla spent the next half hour gushing over the colorful brochures that Isabelle gave her. They had archery, skeet shooting, river rafting, fishing, biking, miles of hiking trails, and of course horseback riding. Kayla wanted to do it all. On top of all of the activities at the ranch, Isabelle told her that there were a lot of attractions to check out in town as well.

"Are you doing a trail ride this morning?" asked Kayla.

"No, I'm not, but one of our wranglers will be. Let me grab him and I'll see if he has room for one more."

"Thanks Isabelle!"

Kayla finished off the last bits of her delicious breakfast. She really wanted seconds, but decided that being super stuffed so early in the morning wasn't a good idea. As good as those biscuits were, they wouldn't be great if she was supposed to get on a horse in the next hour.

Isabelle returned a few minutes later. "You're good to go, follow me."

Kayla followed her out to the stables. There were already six people, two of them young children, mounted on horses. Kayla had never ridden a horse before, but she decided that she could probably keep up with this crowd.

"Kayla, I'd like you to meet George Walters, one of our most experienced wranglers. He's leading the trail ride this morning."

"Howdy miss," he said, tipping his hat.

Kayla felt her cheeks flush. Was he a *real* cowboy? He sure looked like one. He talked like one, too.

"Good morning," she said in what she thought would be a cute voice, but ended up sounding dorky.

"I hear you'll be joining us for a ride today."

Kayla realized that she was smiling too widely. "Yes, I hope it's okay that I've never ridden before."

"You look like a natural," he said with a dazzling white smile.

Kayla felt a butterfly take off in her stomach. His accent would be the death of her. "Oh, I don't know about that."

"Are you ready to find out? Do you trust me?"

Kayla felt the urge to giggle, but luckily was able to resist. Isabelle should've warned her that the wrangler wasn't some grizzled old man, but this stunningly charming cowboy. Did she trust him? She'd follow him off a cliff at this moment.

"Of course," she replied casually.

This vacation was turning out better than she could have ever hoped. He winked at her and turned back into the stables, motioning for her to follow. She practically skipped after him. No need to keep the man waiting.

Chapter 7

When Mitch first arrived at his new place, it looked kind of rough. He blamed it on the poor lighting and the late hour, and went to bed. The next morning, Mitch woke up early, hoping the brilliant sunlight would improve the state of his new rental.

It didn't.

The laminate flooring in the kitchen peeled at the corners. The fridge looked ancient and refused to turn on; he worried that it was either plugged into a bad plug or that it was totally broken. The bathroom was small with pink tiles on the floor and up onto the walls, and the bathtub sported rust all over.

It wasn't like Mitch expected to live in luxury or anything, but it seemed like almost nothing in this house was in working order. When he left Virginia, he was able to take a lot of his tools, but not all of them. Some were damaged in the fire.

He didn't mind fixing things up, but he wasn't sure how much modification he could do since he didn't own the place. He'd have to talk to Marshal Turner about buying something nicer. He had some money saved up, and the FBI was supposed to help him sell his old place back in Virginia. When that went through, he could probably afford something better.

Mitch decided not to worry about that for now and instead focus on his new job. The Marshals arranged for some training on his role as an insurance salesmen. It was hardly a dream come true, but it was a way to earn a living. They said he had six months of salary from the US government before he had to earn his own income; he hoped it wouldn't take him more than a few weeks to figure things out. Though he hated working at a computer, and he knew nothing about insurance, he wanted to give it his best effort.

He spent as much time as he could looking over some of the training documents and trying to familiarize himself with the computer programs. Two hours was all that he could stomach. Not only was it boring, but it hurt his back to sit at a desk so long.

His discomfort was easier to ignore when his stomach wasn't rumbling – he decided that he should head into town and grab something to eat. He was supposed to meet up with Kayla that after-noon anyway for their first meeting. Mitch figured that he might as well get familiar with downtown Cody.

It was a gorgeous day and the wild blue sky almost made him forget that he dragged an innocent bystander into witness protection with him. His first meeting with Kayla didn't go as hoped, to say the least. In his head, he imagined that he'd get the chance to thank her for saving his dad's life and that he'd apologize for how her life was being disrupted. Instead, he insulted her within earshot.

After his poorly timed comment, he held onto the hope that she hadn't heard him. He felt too ashamed to speak to her the rest of dinner, yet she acted like everything was fine. Maybe everything was fine and she didn't hear what he said?

Mitch decided to stop dwelling on it. He found a place to grab a light breakfast and took a seat at the window, watching the activity of the town. There were a lot of people milling about; it seemed like a lot of them were tourists. On the one hand, it helped him blend in. But on the other hand, it could also help some unsavory characters blend in, too.

After he finished eating, Mitch took some time to walk around town, admiring the charm of the various shops and restaurants. He stumbled onto the Buffalo Bill Center of the West and spent the next four hours exploring the museums. He found the history of the area fascinating. He felt like he could stay there all day, and in fact, he'd much prefer that to facing Kayla again.

The time came, though, to meet at a place called Pizza Fantastico. Mitch made sure to get to the restaurant fifteen minutes before their four o'clock meeting time. He ordered a soda and settled in. Four o'clock came and went.

About half an hour passed, he started to get nervous. Maybe something happened to her? Maybe she never made it to the ranch the night before? As he sat there debating what to do, his phone rang. It was Marshal Turner.

"Hello?"

"Hey Mitch, You got a second to talk?"

Mitch felt a tightness in his chest. Something must've happened. "Yeah, what's up?"

"Nothing too exciting, but just wanted to let you know that Kayla's workplace is under surveillance. They found her identity pretty quickly, so it seems like we got her out of there at just the right time."

"Oh, okay. Well that's...good?"

"Yeah, nothing to worry about, we expected this. They haven't gone inside yet to make contact, but one of their guys did call asking for her. Colin Cragin. He's a known entity to us, a fixer for a lot of these white collar guys."

Mitch said nothing, eyeing the pizza shop employee who came out to restock the soda cooler.

Turner continued. "Listen, I figured you'd be with Kayla right now for your meeting, can you let her know?"

"I'm still waiting for her – but yeah, I'll let her know. Should we be on the lookout here for...him?"

"Yeah," he replied. "Always. We don't expect him to find her, but, you know."

"Right."

At that moment, Kayla walked through the door.

"Hey, I gotta go. Kayla just got here."

"Sure – call if you need anything."

The line cut out.

"Sorry I'm late," Kayla said, taking a seat across from him. "Our trail ride this morning went a little long."

Mitch felt the tension leave his body – thank goodness nothing happened to her. "It's alright, I was just starting to get worried that someone – "

Kayla laughed. "All that happened was that one of the horses got spooked by a snake and took off. Took us half an hour to track her down. George, our guide, said that it was a younger horse. I think he regretted bringing her out."

"I bet," said Mitch. She was distracted with the menu, so he had a moment to look at her.

Despite having some dirt on her face and her hair being all messy, she was really pretty. Maybe even more so than he first realized. What puzzled him was how she managed to get involved in some type of group activity the first morning of being in Cody. He didn't know how to ask that without being rude, though, so he didn't say anything.

"So," she said, setting down the menu. "Want to split a pizza?"

"Sure. But first, I need to tell you something."

"Okay?"

He took a deep breath. "I got a call from – uh, Mr. Turner. Our friend."

She nodded. "Uh huh, I know the guy."

"He wanted me to let you know that...uh." Mitch dropped his voice low. "Your workplace is under surveillance by a guy named – "

Kayla cut him off with a tut. "I don't want to know! La la la!"

Mitch pulled back, puzzled.

She continued. "As long as nothing is wrong," she paused, looking at him expectantly.

He shook his head. "No, nothing's wrong, but I think you should know that – "

"Then I don't want to know any details. I trust Mr. Turner to handle it."

Mitch sat back in the booth. How odd. He was so anxious about this new development that he wanted to pack up and run. He wasn't actually going to go, of course, but the instinct hit him. Fight or flight. And Mitch definitely wasn't one to fight. How could she be so casual about it all?

"Alright," she said with a smile. "Let me know if anything changes, but otherwise, I don't want to worry needlessly. What kind of pizza do you like?"

He shrugged. "It doesn't matter."

"I like pepperoni, but I'm not picky."

Mitch liked pepperoni too, but it always gave him heartburn.

"Sounds good to me," he said before getting up to place an order at the counter.

He returned to his seat and silently tried to think of something to say. He never had the talent of talking to people that he didn't know; he worried about saying the wrong thing. It was one of the many differences between him and his father. His dad could talk to anyone about anything, and by the end they would like him, trust him, and probably even give him some money.

Mitch was never like that, and truthfully never wanted to be. His mom was not a smooth talker – she didn't need to be, because she never did anything wrong and didn't need to manipulate people. Though she had her own charm once you got to know her, it wasn't something that caught people right away. Because of his dad, Mitch always distrusted charming people.

Kayla eventually broke the silence. "So, are you staying on a ranch too?"

"No," said Mitch. "Not a Ranch. A rental house."

"Is it nice?"

Mitch paused. He couldn't think of a single thing that would count as nice, but he didn't want to seem like a complainer. "Yeah, it's pretty nice."

Kayla nodded. "That's good. The ranch that I'm staying at is nice too. It's called New Morning Ranch, and it's owned by this guy and his daughter. It seems like a pretty big operation. I have to ask later how many people are staying there..."

She looked up, as though she were adding that to an invisible list of tasks in her head.

"There are a lot of cool activities there, too. Like, I did the horse-back riding today – I definitely think I want to do that again, it was my first time on a horse. It was harder than I expected, but we had a little picnic and overall it was amazing to see everything on horse-back. I'm guessing you don't have anything like that out by you?"

Mitch laughed. "No, it's pretty much just me and then nothing for miles."

"Oh," she said, waving a hand. "Well that's no fun. I'm sure you could tag along on some of my stuff. We could make it one of our... meetings."

"Sure."

She continued. "I'm not sure if you would be interested in all of them, but I mean, definitely some of them. Like maybe the archery, river rafting, or fishing? I'm actually not terribly into fishing, but if you really want to do that we could."

Mitch nodded. "There's lots of stuff in town, too. There's a rodeo. And did you see the Buffalo Bill museum?"

"A rodeo!" she excitedly slapped a hand on the table. "That sounds awesome. I didn't get to walk around town yet. But what's up with everything being named after Buffalo Bill? Wasn't he like a movie star?"

Mitch forced himself not to laugh or even smile at her comment. "Well...I don't know about the movie star thing. But his name was Colonel William Frederick 'Buffalo Bill' Cody."

Kayla narrowed her eyes. "Are you messing with me?"

Mitch shook his head. "No – I learned a lot about him at the museum. He was one of the founders of the city."

"Well that explains a lot," Kayla said, covering her eyes with her hand. "Good thing I learned that now and not with a local."

"That's one way to look at it," replied Mitch. After the words escaped his mouth, he instantly regretted them. What he *meant* to say was that she had a good attitude about the whole thing. But the way he said it instead sounded like he was being judgmental.

The moment passed, though, and Kayla didn't seem to flinch. Maybe it didn't come across that way. He knew he'd be replaying it in his head all night.

The pizza came out that moment, and it was much bigger than expected. After eating their fill, there was still half of it left. Mitch wanted Kayla to take it with her, but she refused.

"All of my meals are included at the ranch. After seeing what they made for breakfast, I have a feeling that it'll all be really good."

"Are you sure?"

"Thank you, but I'm sure." She stood up. "Let's grab the check and get going?"

Mitch closed the pizza box. "Oh, I already took care of it."

She frowned. "Alright, I'll get it next time."

They left the restaurant and walked down the sidewalk.

Mitch dropped his voice. "I never got a chance to thank you for saving my dad. And to tell you how sorry I am that you're stuck here. Just to make sure that we discuss this too – has anything concerning happened to you since you got here?"

"Nope," replied Kayla. "Everything's been great so far. And don't worry about it."

He tried to think of how to reply but she was already onto the next topic.

"Oh! Look at this."

Mitch leaned to look at the telephone pole in front of her. There was a sign on it for a fundraiser.

"It's for a couple whose house was destroyed by a tornado! I thought those almost *never* happen out here. That's so sad," she said.

"I don't think it's terribly uncommon here."

She tapped her chin. "So sad. I think I'll go to this."

That seemed like an odd choice. Mitch didn't want to go anywhere where there might be a lot of attention. He still felt skittish about his new identity.

"Well," he said, "I think I'd better get back to work."

She turned to face him. "What work?"

He sighed. "I'm supposed to learn how to be an insurance sales-man for my new...well, you know."

"That's rough," she said. "Alright, well I'll see you later."

"Definitely," he said. "I'm looking forward to it!"

Chapter 8

Looking forward to seeing her again?

Kayla felt like she was torturing the man by talking at him for the last hour. There was no way that he was genuinely looking forward to seeing her again.

"Have a good day!" she said, turning to walk away.

It was odd. When she first met Mitch, she thought he was kind of cute. He had that tall, dark, and brooding thing going on.

But after he insulted her, she was over it. Brooding was one thing, being rude was another. Maybe he didn't plan to have anyone tag along with him to Wyoming, but that was no reason to be mean. She couldn't help that she got pulled into this!

And she definitely wasn't dumb, like he insinuated – she just wasn't a criminal like him. He was probably blindingly rich from all of the fraud that landed him in witness protection in the first place. Rich people always think everyone else is stupid. It wasn't *her* problem that he was a snob.

The one thing she did feel a bit silly about was not knowing that Buffalo Bill was a real person. Why did she admit that to him? Probably because she was nervous. Whenever she could tell that someone didn't like her, it made her talk a mile a minute. Plus, she had this terrible habit of needing to fill silence. The result was often something silly coming out of her mouth.

At the same time, if she hadn't said anything, they would've sat, staring at each other, and not speaking a word. That would've been suspicious! Someone might think they were an unhappy couple or something and start asking questions. No need to pique everyone's interest by being weird and sullen.

She decided not to let his snobbery ruin her Wild West vacation. Her horseback ride that morning was incredible. It was a little scary when that horse ran off with the little girl on its back, but it didn't cause any harm.

Also, George was *very* good on horseback. Not just good looking – that bit was distracting – he was also quite skilled. He told her that he worked at a different ranch every season because he liked to travel the country and see all that life had to offer.

Kayla was impressed with his outlook – he was probably one of the most skilled wranglers in the area because he'd been to so many places.

She was also impressed with his Southern gentleman accent from growing up in Georgia. She felt like she could listen to him all day – and that was the real reason she was late to meet Mitch. She offered to help George take the saddles off of the horses, even though she had no idea how long that would take or what it entailed. In her opinion, she couldn't spend a month at a ranch and not at least learn how to take care of horses!

She made a mental note to be better about being on time, though. No need to annoy Mitch any more than necessary. Also, she made a note on her phone for the time and place of the fundraiser for the tornado family. She wanted to be sure that she attended, to see if she could help in any way and to get to know the people in town.

Kayla slowly wandered through the streets, admiring the beautiful backdrop. Her goal was to make it all the way down Sheridan Avenue to the Buffalo Bill Museum so she wouldn't say anything else ditzy about Cody. The problem was that she kept getting distracted with the side streets and the little shops along the way. She was a sucker for tourist trinkets, but she reminded herself that she wasn't here to fill up her suitcase with junk.

After an hour of perusing the shops, she was much closer to buying a cowgirl hat than she was to walking into the museum. She truly wanted to learn the history of the area (and not just to look smart in front of Mitch), but she also felt like a cowgirl hat was equally important for fitting in. Come to think of it, though, she didn't see many people wearing hats. Maybe they were all tourists too? Was it dorky to get a hat?

She debated the merits of the hat and settled on at least buying a book about the history of Cody – it had a lot of neat pictures that would be fun to show her parents once she got back home. She tucked the book into her purse and decided that she needed to get serious about making it to the museum before it closed.

Unfortunately for her plans, the next store she passed was a pet store and she was immediately distracted by a little yellow dog.

"Hi there sweetie!" Kayla knelt down to get a better look at the adorable face hiding under the bench.

The dog pretended that he couldn't see her – looking up, around, and any way but at her.

"You just look like you want to melt into the ground and disappear," said Kayla gently, slowly offering the back of her hand to the dog to smell.

"That's because he does," beamed a voice behind her.

Kayla stood up. "Oh I'm so sorry, is this your dog?"

He nodded and crossed his arms. "Unfortunately, it is."

Kayla didn't know how to respond to that. "Sorry, I'm being so rude. My name is Kayla. I'm staying at the New Morning Ranch for a few weeks."

"Is that right? Staying with the Connors?"

She nodded. "Yeah!"

"Nice to meet you Kayla, I'm Butch. That's good to hear. They're good people."

"Nice to meet you, Butch."

Butch looked down at his dog. "Yeah, I tied him out here hoping someone would come by and want to take him off my hands."

Kayla tried to hide the shock on her face, but did a poor job of it. "Oh?"

"Look at him," he said extending a hand. "He's a healthy dog, don't get me wrong. But he's just – my daughter brought him to me, after she found him wandering around. She thought I could get some use out of him at the farm, either hunting or protecting some of the chickens."

"Ah. And he's...not been a very good worker?"

"No!" Butch said, taking off his ball cap and rubbing his forehead. "He's afraid of everything, most of all me, and he sulks around like the world's coming after him."

Kayla squatted again to look at him. The dog was still firmly avoiding any and all eye contact. "Maybe he didn't have the best life before your daughter found him."

Butch sighed. "Yeah, that's what I'm thinking. And I'm sorry for it, but I don't have the time or the patience to deal with a skittish dog."

"Aw," said Kayla. "But he's so pretty!"

A smile spread across Butch's face. "Sounds like you two might be a match."

Kayla laughed. "I've always wanted a dog, but I don't know that right now is the right time."

Butch pulled his hat back on and sighed. "That's what I've been running into. My buddy owns this pet shop, and he thought that I might be able to find someone to take him. But it's summer now, and the town is full of tourists. Nobody wants to bring a dog home with them."

Kayla shifted her weight. He was probably right. Most people don't go on vacation and have a contingency plan for getting a new dog. Then again, what better time to get a dog than when she didn't have any real responsibilities...

"What are you going to do with him?" she asked.

Butch kneeled down to pat the dog's head. "I don't know. Maybe drop him off in Jackson and see if some celebrity will take him on."

"In Jackson Hole?"

"Yeah, you ever been there?"

"No, but I've heard of it," she replied.

"It's a great place if you want to pay twice as much to hang around a bunch of rich Californians."

Kayla didn't know what that was about, but it wasn't her battle to fight. "Is he house trained?"

Butch shrugged. "Dunno. I've only had him a few weeks, I've been keeping him in the barn. He doesn't like that, though, and he's gotten out a bunch of times."

Kayla looked down at the dog again. "So you don't like barns, and you don't like strangers. What do you like little fella?"

The dog turned his head towards her and inched his body closer. He extended his nose to sniff her hand. Excited, Kayla slowly lowered herself until she was sitting on the sidewalk next to him. He took one heavy paw and set it on her thigh.

Kayla felt her heart swell. "Look, he likes me!"

"Huh, would you look at that."

She extended her hand to delicately stroke the fur on his back. He did not resist.

"Hm," she said out loud. "Here's the thing. I'll be up at the ranch for the next few weeks. I don't know if dogs are allowed."

He shrugged. "They probably are."

She shot him a smile. Of course he would say that. Though...it wouldn't hurt to give the ranch a call and just ask them. If they said no, that was that. And if they said yes – well then she had a decision to make.

She *did* always want a dog. But much like the other plans in her life, everything took a backseat to her becoming a doctor. While she was in school, she spent countless hours studying at the library. Once she went into residency, there were days that she had 24 hour shifts at the hospital. It would have been unfair for her to have a dog then.

But what was holding her back now? This was supposed to be the beginning of her new life. This dog clearly needed a new life, too. Plus, he seemed to like her. And she couldn't take her eyes off of him.

The thought of walking away from this living, breathing creature to walk around a museum filled with dead stuff felt intolerable. She could visit the museum anytime, and she could just avoid talking to anyone about Buffalo Bill until she had the chance. Plus, she got that history book! That would catch her right up. She could even read it to her new dog!

"I can see the wheels turning in your head," Butch said. "I don't want to put any pressure on you, but my friend Lincoln owns the pet shop. I'm sure he'd give you a nice discount on supplies if I told him you were taking this dog off of my hands."

Kayla smiled. If she spent some time thinking, she could certainly come up with reasons why this was a bad idea. But she didn't want to do that. It felt right.

"Butch, you've got yourself a deal!"

He stuck out his hand for a handshake. "And I thought I'd be sitting out here all week."

She paused. "Do you mind if I go inside and get some of the supplies now?"

"Go right ahead. Tell Lincoln you're taking the dog."

Kayla made a quick call to the ranch – it turned out dogs were allowed for a small additional fee. She walked into the pet shop and found Lincoln, the only person in the store, tending to the fish tanks. He was pleasantly surprised to hear that she was going to take Butch's dog.

"I confess though," she told him, "that I've never had a dog before, so I'm not sure what I'm supposed to get."

"I'm happy to help you with that," Lincoln said.

They spent the next half hour going around the store to pick up things that she would need. It didn't seem like Lincoln was taking her for a ride, at least; and with everything, he told her that she could take it or leave it. The only thing that he insisted she needed was a good leash that the dog couldn't escape from, and a bag of food.

"The rest is all your preference," he said.

He showed her a book that would help her through owning her first dog. It talked about obedience training, house training, and even using a crate to train the dog.

"Isn't that cruel?" she asked. "To put him in a cage?"

Lincoln shook his head. "No ma'am. All of my dogs are crate trained. Keeps them out of trouble when I'm not home. You don't plan on keeping him in there all the time, do you?"

"No, of course not."

"Good. It'll be like a den for him. That way, he can learn the rules of the house and not destroy anything that he shouldn't while you're away."

By the end of it, Kayla decided to buy everything that Lincoln showed her. It wasn't terribly expensive, plus he was giving her a discount. She left with a large crate, an elevated set of bowls, a pack of tennis balls, a dog bed, three squeaky toys, a no slip leash, and a handful of other things that she thought looked cute. Lincoln even had a machine to make a dog tag right in the store.

"Do you know what you're going to name him? We can make that up for you right now."

"I didn't even think about it!" she said.

"Let me ring you up, maybe something will come to you."

She stood there, racking her brain for a good name. Pongo? No, that was from a movie...was it the dalmatian movie? She couldn't use that.

Marty popped into her head. That was cute!

Oh wait, definitely couldn't use that – that was the name of the criminal that she wasn't supposed to know. She couldn't very well name her dog after him. Plus, he didn't look like a Marty. He looked sad, like a...like a what? He was a dog getting kicked off of a farm. A dog that liked to escape. A dog that was basically an orphan. Like Oliver Twist!

She remembered reading that book when she was in school, but she was fuzzy on the details. Was it offensive to name her dog after a Dickens character?

"You ready with that name?"

She decided that no one needed to know where the name came from. "Yes! I'm going with Oliver."

"Sounds good to me. Write out your name and phone number so I can put it on the tag. In case he gets loose."

"Okay!" Kayla couldn't believe this was actually happening. Her first dog! Sure, it wasn't the best timing. When her vacation here was done, she'd have to convince Perez to let Oliver on the plane home. It wouldn't be a big deal. If worse came to worst, she could just drive back to New York with her new friend in tow.

Kayla made sure to write down her fake name and paid for all of the supplies. She asked Lincoln if he'd hang on to them for a second while she pulled her car up to the shop.

"No problem," he said. "I'm happy to help you with that."

Before she knew it, her car was full of supplies and Butch was untying Oliver's leash from the bench. She was a bit nervous that he wouldn't want to get in the car with her, but as soon as she clicked her tongue, he jumped into the backseat. Impressed, she shut the door and scurried over to the driver's seat. She waved goodbye to Lincoln and Butch before turning on the engine.

"Alright Oliver, it's just you and me. Are you ready to see your new home?"

He sat up, panting nervously and breathing hot, stinky dog breath into her face.

"Whew we need to get you some water, and maybe some doggy mints, but I'll take that as a yes!" She put the car into drive and headed back to the ranch.

Chapter 9

Over the next few days, Mitch replayed his conversation with Kayla in his head. He had a hard time meeting new people; it was difficult for him to make conversation, and then afterwards he worried that what he said could be taken as offensive or rude.

It wasn't the best quality for someone starting over in life, but that's who he was. As he got to know Kayla, he would open up more. He wasn't the kind of guy to tell just anyone his life story. He certainly didn't mind sharing a pizza with her, though; there were much worse ways to spend an afternoon – like reading about insurance.

Yet that's exactly what he needed to focus on before he would see her again. They were supposed to meet up again in three days, and Mitch felt like he had a lot that he needed to accomplish before then.

First, he needed to assess what actually worked in his rental house. His landlord agreed to take a look at the fridge, so that was a good start.

There were also the issues of a dripping kitchen faucet, the wonky toilet, peeling floors, and various other little annoyances that he found around the house. He spent a full day fixing things himself – replacing light bulbs, tightening door knobs, fixing leaks and generally cleaning the place up. It seemed like no one had lived there in ages. He wondered how much the Marshals were paying for this place.

The next day was dedicated to studying the insurance salesman manual. It was dull reading. He appreciated that the Marshals found a job for him that he can do without going back to school, but at the same time, he dreaded every minute of it. The thought of actually talking to people to convince them to buy insurance made him want to hide under his desk. It was only *slightly* better than going back to Virginia to face the goons himself.

Mitch understood that people needed to insure their cars and homes, of course. He just didn't know how to be a salesman. It was totally against his nature. The training book said to suggest other types of insurance that might be useful to a customer. While he had no problem suggesting something that might benefit them, he wouldn't push them if they said no. And he'd never offer something people didn't need. He wondered if he'd be able to make a living without being pushy.

Slightly disheartened, he spent the next day driving around and buying supplies to fix up his house. He could fix almost anything, and if he didn't know how to fix it, he'd find it on the internet and figure it out. He liked working with his hands. Working on a computer was just...boring. He wished he could get back into wood-working, but the Marshals were clear about that; trying to work as a carpenter again would run the risk of attracting too much attention.

Mitch was relieved when it was finally time to see Kayla again. The morning before their meeting time, she sent him a text asking if he would mind swinging by the ranch that afternoon instead of meeting her in town. He didn't mind meeting her at the ranch, but he worried that it might be unwise. What if there was someone staying there keeping an eye on her, waiting to see if she made contact with him?

After expressing his concerns, she replied with a text saying, "I don't think any of the families or the two sets of newlyweds pose any risk to my safety."

He knew that she was probably right, but he wanted to be careful. He decided he'd go to the ranch early and scope out any suspicious characters. The Marshals sent him pictures of Colin, the goon who apparently was on the lookout for Kayla. Mitch would make sure he hadn't found his way to Cody somehow.

At six, he got into his pickup truck to make the drive. It felt like he drove for miles without seeing another soul before all of a sudden, a beautiful wooden sign appeared for the ranch. He pulled onto the dusty road and followed it until he reached a parking lot.

Kayla was right; the ranch was a big operation. Although there wasn't much in terms of livestock roaming around, there was a very impressive stable standing in the distance.

From the looks of it, he didn't see any suspicious people lurking around. Like Kayla said, it was mostly families with kids and a few younger looking couples.

He got out of his truck and admired the mountains in the backdrop; as he stood there, he got a few friendly "hello's" and "howdy's" and a young woman approached him.

"Hi there," she said. "Can I help you find something?"

"Oh hi," he replied. "I was looking for a friend. Her name is Kayla?"

"Sure, I'll show you to her cabin."

That was a little too easy. Mitch made a mental note to mention it to Kayla and followed the young woman down a winding path.

No wonder Kayla was able to get into fun activities so early in her stay; this ranch was full of life. It was a stark contrast to the past three days he spent alone in his dilapidated house. It seemed like solitary confinement compared to this.

They arrived at a cozy looking cabin. The young woman led him to the front door and knocked. Mitch heard some shuffling inside before Kayla's voice called out, "Just a second!"

A moment later, Kayla cracked open the door. Her cheeks were a bit flushed. "Hey Isabelle, what's up?"

"You've got a visitor. Is everything okay in there?"

Kayla popped her head out further and spotted Mitch. "Oh, is it time already? Sorry! Thanks so much Isabelle, and yeah, everything is fine."

"Okay, have a good evening!"

Mitch took a step towards the front door. "Hi, how are you?"

Kayla watched as Isabelle descended the front porch steps and disappeared down the pathway. "Quick," she whispered, "get inside."

Startled, Mitch obeyed. "Is someone coming after you?"

Kayla shut the door behind him. "No," she said impatiently. "I just have a little bit of a situation going on."

"What kind of situation?"

Before she could say anything else, a large dog came charging from the back of the cabin, barking fiercely. Mitch didn't flinch. His mom was a huge animal lover, as was he, and he always had dogs growing up.

"Hey fella," he said, dropping to one knee. "What're you so upset about?"

"He really doesn't like men," said Kayla nervously. "It's okay Oliver, he's not here to hurt you."

The dog continued barking at him with growls intermingled. Mitch made sure not to look him in the eyes as he sat still.

Oliver stopped barking and sniffed his arm.

"We're not all bad," said Mitch.

"How did you do that?" asked Kayla, hands on her hips. "He almost ate George the other day when he stopped by. I was afraid I couldn't let anyone in here again."

"Dogs like me," said Mitch. He kept his voice low and made sure not to move as Oliver investigated him. "And I like dogs. As much as I would like to pet him, I don't think he's ready for that yet."

Kayla grabbed Oliver by the collar and pulled him into a hug. "I don't think he is, and I don't want him to change his mind and try to eat you, too."

After a few seconds, Mitch stood up and got a good look at the cabin. Yep – it was definitely a lot nicer than where he was staying. He was glad. Kayla deserved a decent place.

"Is he...one of the ranch dogs?" asked Mitch.

"No," Kayla said, standing up. "He's mine. I got him from a farmer who didn't want him. We're working through some issues right now, and currently I'm not accepting any opinions on the matter, so you can save it."

"Okay!" Mitch replied. He almost took a step back from the forcefulness of her words. Cleary this was a sensitive topic. Or she expected him to say something offensive. He felt dread rise in his chest – maybe she did hear what he said about her to Agent Simmons that first night.

"Now," she continued, "I planned for us to go fly fishing today, but I can't leave him alone here. He's developed some...destructive tendencies." She motioned to a wooden chair that was turned on its side.

Mitch knelt down to get a better look. It looked like one of the legs was chewed clean off. He found it lying nearby.

"I see that," he said. "I may be able to fix this. Do you mind if I take this leg with me?"

Kayla rubbed her forehead. "Sure, it's not doing much good now."

"Alright."

He didn't care about going fishing, but he'd spent the last three days entirely alone and he didn't want to miss out on spending some time with her. Of course he couldn't admit that, though. She wasn't his biggest fan.

"Maybe we could take him for a hike? Burn off some energy?" he suggested.

Kayla shrugged. She looked defeated. "Yeah, I guess we can try that."

"It'll be good," Mitch said, trying to brighten his tone. "The first week or two is always tough with a rescue dog. You both need time to adjust."

She gave him a suspicious look. "You know dogs?"

"A bit," he said.

As if on cue, Oliver trotted by, squeaking a toy in his mouth.

"I thought it'd come more naturally," Kayla said, watching him disappear into another room. "But it seems like I'm just a bad dog owner."

"I promise you're not a bad dog owner," Mitch said. "Oliver – are you ready to go for a walk?"

Oliver blasted into the room, his eyes darting between them both.

Kayla shot Mitch a surprised look. "I think he understood you."

Mitch smiled. "He did. Someone taught him that word. Ready to go?"

She sighed. "Sure, let's see how this goes." Kayla grabbed his leash and turned to leave.

Finally, Mitch felt like he could be of some use. He didn't know how to make conversation, and he didn't know how to sell insurance, but he did know how to make a rescue dog feel at home. Maybe he could help Kayla after all – and maybe, just maybe, she'd forgive him for being a jerk.

Chapter 10

After clipping on Oliver's leash, Kayla hurriedly walked him through the front door. She didn't want Mitch to see that she was annoyed. She didn't want to deal with Mitch at all, actually. He probably thought it was dumb of her to take in a wild dog like Oliver. But she wasn't interested in his opinion. She felt silly enough as it was.

The first night with Oliver went well – in hindsight, Kayla realized that it lulled her into a false sense of security. She got him to the cabin and he trotted from room to room, sniffing and wagging his tail.

At first, it seemed like he was quite pleased with his new digs. Kayla unpacked his stuff, set up his bowls, laid out his bed, and provided him with some toys. She figured out how to set up the crate and dragged the bed inside. He wasn't interested in going in right away, but that made sense. She assumed it would take some treats and bribery to get him to accept the crate.

She fed him dinner that night, which he ate heartily, and as soon as he was done, he went to the front door and peed on it. She rushed over and managed to get him out the door before he did too much damage. After that, he seemed to understand that he had to be on the *other* side of the door to go potty. Most of the time, at least.

There were some other issues that emerged over the next two days. First, Oliver didn't seem to like any other dogs. Whenever Kayla took him out for a walk, he would bark and lunge at the other dogs as though they insulted him in some way.

The ranch dogs just stood and stared at him, almost as if they were amused by his wild behavior. Kayla was *not* amused, but she didn't know how to get it to stop. He almost pulled her over one time – she was surprised by how strong he was.

He cowered when he saw men (especially men in hats), so she was particularly startled with his aggressive barking when George knocked on her door. He barked so ferociously that he even peed a little on the floor, and Kayla was afraid to invite George in.

This was all okay, though. She figured that she'd need to teach him some manners. What was not okay was the surprise Kayla had when she came home from breakfast the third day that she had him.

For the first two days, she brought him with her wherever she went. For food, she'd grab something quickly so he wasn't left alone in the cabin. After two days, though, he seemed to be pretty well-behaved, and since he wouldn't go into his crate without barking and crying, she figured she could leave him for 30 minutes to have breakfast and catch up with Isabelle and George.

When she returned to the cabin, he came trotting over, wagging his tail and celebrating her return.

"Hey buddy!" she said happily. Then the smell hit her.

"Oh my goodness," she said, almost gagging. "What is that?"

She had a hard time locating it, mainly because everywhere she turned, she found more destruction. The first thing that caught her eye were the mountains of white fluff that Oliver ripped out of his dog bed. It was utterly destroyed, its innards strewn around the cabin.

Next she saw that he chewed the wooden chair leg off. She wandered into the kitchen and let out a gasp – somehow he managed to get up to the counter, open the breadbox, and eat an entire loaf of bread. The paper bag that previously contained it was ripped to bits.

In her bedroom, she discovered the chewed and destroyed cowboy boots that the wardrobe girls specifically picked out for her "in case of cowgirl emergency." The carpet was wet – she looked down and realized that he spilled his entire bowl of water.

His crowning achievement, though, was the surprise that he left for her atop the bed. Apparently, eating an entire loaf of bread really gets a dog moving.

She stood there feeling totally stunned.

"What have I done?" she said to no one. "They're going to kick me out, and then the Marshals will kick me out of WITSEC and the FBI will prosecute me. And it's all my fault for bringing home this wild dog."

Following Kayla's lackluster response to his greeting, Oliver became a bit confused and decided to take a seat a few feet away from her, staring nervously.

It was then that Kayla asked Mitch if he would be willing to change their meeting place. She needed the rest of the day to clean up the mess that Oliver made.

Kayla tried to push the memory of the morning out of her mind to enjoy the hike. She took a deep breath – the air was so fresh that it helped soothe her nostrils, which were still a bit sensitive from all of the bleach she'd used cleaning.

"Do you have a map with any hiking trails?" asked Mitch.

Shoot. She didn't, and she wished that she had the time to plan something short so she wouldn't have to spend too long with Mitch. She wanted to go back to the cabin and feel sorry for herself. "No, but I'm sure that they have some in the lodge."

Oliver caught sight of a squirrel twenty yards away. His body stiffened and he started slowly creeping up on the creature. Even though she was still mad at him, she couldn't help but crack a smile. Adopting him was probably the most irresponsible thing she'd done in some time – and she was infamous for her spur of the moment bad ideas. He was so stinking cute, though. How could she have known that she would be such a terrible dog owner?

"I could run in and get a map for us," said Mitch.

"Sure, that sounds –"

Kayla was interrupted by a lovely Southern accent.

"Hey there Miss Smith."

She turned around and there was George, all ruggedly handsome, squinting into the sun.

"Oh hi George, what's up?"

"Just finished up my last trail ride for the day. What are you up to?"

He took a step closer and Oliver let out a low grumble.

"Ollie!" Kayla said. "Stop being rude! I'm sorry, he's still a bit afraid of men."

"That's alright pup," George said, reaching down to pat him on the head.

Oliver's grumbling intensified into a growl and Kayla tugged on his leash.

She got low to scold him. "Oliver – no!"

Oliver stopped growling, but didn't break his stare with George.

"That's alright," George said. "I like a dog with a little fight in him."

"He has a lot of fight," Kayla said with a sigh. She knelt down to stroke Oliver's head and soft little ears. "George, this is my friend Mitch. And Mitch, this is George, one of the wranglers at the ranch."

Mitch outstretched a hand. "Nice to meet you, George."

Kayla continued. "We were thinking of taking Oliver on a little hike. Do you have any recommendations?"

George crossed his arms. "Well I'd be happy to show you one. I couldn't leave a lovely lady like you out to fend for yourself in these grizzly infested mountains."

Kayla was glad that her cheeks were already a bit pink from the heat so George didn't see her growing flushed. This day was looking up after all!

"I'm sure we can manage," said Mitch.

"If you don't have anything else to do, of course you're welcome to join us," added Kayla quickly. She wasn't going to miss the chance of hanging out with George. Especially if he could be a bit of a buffer between her and Mitch. What did Mitch care? He didn't like talking to her anyway.

"As luck would have it, I'm free the rest of the evening."

"Great! Where should we go?"

For the next hour, George led them through a series of winding trails and foot paths. Kayla found it absolutely enchanting, and even Oliver eventually set aside his distrust of George to pursue the many exciting sites and smells of the countryside.

Kayla's cover story was that she lived in New York City, so she made a big deal about how beautiful and open everything was compared to "home." Though it felt a bit dishonest, especially since she'd only been to the city a handful of times, it was mostly true. The mountains and blue skies took her breath away. She wasn't much of a city person; everything from the traffic and the crowding and the buildings made her feel claustrophobic. It moved too fast for her liking, too. She felt more at home driving from one little rural clinic to another.

"Isabelle's been going on all week about how cool it is that you're from New York City," George commented.

Kayla let out a laugh. "It's not that great," she said before thinking.

"Oh, you don't like it?" said Mitch, a smile tugging at the corners of his mouth.

Kayla shot him a look. He knew she wasn't really from New York City. Was he trying to get her to blow her cover again?

"I mainly moved there for work, but I don't want to live there forever. I don't really feel at home in big cities," Kayla replied, keeping her face forward.

The last part was entirely true. If Mitch wanted her to say something dumb, she wasn't going to fall for it. She was getting good at this lying thing.

"I could never live in a city," responded George. "The way I see it, a real man is like a horse. He needs wide skies and open fields to run in, to feel his own strength."

"Yeah," sighed Kayla. "It's so much freer out here."

They reached the end of the walk then, the path looping them back into the ranch's parking lot.

"How about we grab some dinner?" said George.

"Oh yeah!" Kayla responded without thinking.

Oliver let out a grumble, as though he just again realized that George was nearby.

"Ah," she said, "except I don't think I can leave Oliver alone tonight. We're working on – uh – some separation anxiety."

"Bring him along. I could order a pizza in town and we could eat it looking up at the stars."

Kayla's eyes caught his for just a moment. Was he...asking her on a date? Sort of? Kind of?

More importantly, was she going to say *yes?*

"That sounds nice," she said cooly.

"I'll be back in a bit," George said with a wink.

Mitch cleared his throat. "Well, I better head off too. Need to get started on some work early tomorrow."

Kayla nodded. "Alright Mitch, have a good night."

He hesitated. "You too. And uh, see you later this week?"

"Sure," Kayla replied.

She wondered if she'd have time to shower and change before George got back. This was her first date in years – it was no good for her to be all sweaty for it. She needed to get moving.

Mitch leaned down to Oliver's level. "Nice meeting you, Ollie."

Oliver sniffed his hand before offering a solitary lick. Mitch laughed.

"I'll take it."

Kayla patted Oliver on the head. "Good boy! See, it's not so hard to be nice, is it?"

Mitch turned to leave. "Let me know if you need anything."

"Will do!" Kayla was finally able to scurry back to her cabin to get ready. Her heart was all aflutter with excitement. Maybe her spontaneous trip out West would lead to a spontaneous cowboy husband?

Chapter 11

He watched as Kayla disappeared down the path to her cabin. If George hadn't joined in on their walk, Mitch would've had a chance to outright ask Kayla if she'd seen anything suspicious, or if anyone came looking for her. Was this Colin guy smart enough to show up at the ranch with a fake family? Probably not. And the Marshals would see that coming.

But George did invite himself on their walk, so Mitch didn't get to check in with Kayla at all.

George. What a guy. "A real man is like a horse."

Mitch snorted. Right. It took everything he had not to burst out laughing when George said that. He wanted to ask him, "How many of these ranch horses are living out in the open fields? Aren't they all technically employees here? Is that also a metaphor for your life as a real man?"

He thought that Kayla would at least roll her eyes at George's statement, but when he looked at her, she was staring off into the sky. It seemed that she found this braggart charming. Mitch didn't know why, but he just didn't like the guy. He had a fake sort of charm that set Mitch's teeth on edge – it reminded him of his dad.

Plus, George was being overly forward with Oliver; even though Oliver was growling at him, he barged in and started petting him. That really annoyed Mitch.

Kayla wasn't sure how to handle Oliver yet, and Mitch didn't blame her. It was her first dog and she was just getting used to everything. She had Oliver's best interest at heart, and Mitch respected her for that. But George acted like an outright fool by ignoring all of Oliver's warnings. He was lucky he wasn't bitten.

Mitch got back to his place and parked his truck. He sat and absorbed the silence for a moment. It would be a few days before he could see Kayla again, and he couldn't count on her to be his only friend. It was about time that he started to make some friends of his own. Once Kayla went back to her regular life, there would be absolutely no one in town that he knew. He needed to put down roots here, because this beautiful place was his future.

A solution sort of fell into his lap the next day when he went to the hardware store. He got into a conversation with an older guy who was gathering materials to build a wheelchair ramp for his wife.

"Our old house was all set up for her, but we lost it in the tornado," he told Mitch.

"Wait a minute," said Mitch. "Are you John Singer?"

"The one and only," he replied.

Mitch laughed. "I saw that there's a fundraiser for you and your wife coming up – a square dance, I think? After the tornado hit your house?"

"Yeah," said John. "That's something our church set up for us. I appreciate what they're trying to do. I just don't know how we'll ever be able to rebuild our home."

"Where are you staying now?"

"We're up with my cousin, but I hate to trespass on his hospitality any longer. I can't believe it, but the insurance had some loophole where we got almost nothing for our house."

Mitch shifted uncomfortably. "Yeah, I sell the stuff and I don't always understand how it works."

John sighed. "Maybe you can find us new insurance that'll help next time."

"I'd be happy to look into it," said Mitch. "But how about today I help you build that ramp?"

"No," John said waving a hand, "I don't want to trouble you."

Mitch insisted. "It'll take you three times as long by yourself, and I've got nothing to do today."

It took the rest of the day to design and build a wheelchair safe ramp. While he was working, he got a text from Kayla asking if he wanted to go fishing later that week.

"We could do that," he responded. "Or I could introduce you to my new friend John Singer – the guy who lost his house in that tornado."

She responded instantly. "What? Are you serious? I would love to meet him, I have some ideas about how to help him and his wife."

"John said that they're all ears."

Later that week, Kayla showed up at Mitch's front door, Oliver in tow.

"Come on in," he said. "I've got something to show you."

Oliver didn't need to be asked twice – Kayla unclipped his leash and he bolted through the door.

"Oh my goodness," she said. "I'm sorry. I can keep him on the leash so he doesn't damage anything."

Mitch shrugged. "There's nothing that he can really damage here that isn't already damaged."

She stopped and looked around the room. "Uh...did the FBI tell the Marshals to punish you?"

"For what?"

"I mean, compared to where I get to stay, this place is – no offense – a dump."

As badly as he wanted to laugh, Mitch was able to keep a straight face. "It is?"

"No, I mean," she said hurriedly, "it's just that, well, I assume that you're used to living with a certain standard, and this place doesn't seem to be up to that kind of standard."

Mitch stared at her for a moment. A certain kind of standard? Did she think that he was rich or something?

Before he could respond, she started talking again. "It's just different than what I imagined. For you."

"For me?" Mitch said with a bemused smile.

"You know what I mean!" Kayla said.

He crossed his arms and leaned against the wall. "Did the Marshals or FBI tell you anything about how I ended up here?"

She frowned. "To be honest, it was all kind of a blur."

Mitch's stare was unbroken. "I'm not in witness protection because of something that I did."

She narrowed her eyes. "So why *are* you in witness protection then?"

Oliver came trotting into the room and hopped onto Mitch's couch. Kayla motioned for him to get down, but Mitch waved a hand. "Don't worry about it, as you can see it's not a nice couch."

"It's a nice couch," she said unconvincingly.

"You really are a terrible liar," Mitch said with a laugh. "It's okay. It came with the place. And it's a long story, but I'm in witness protection because my dad stole a lot of money from a lot of innocent people over the years, and I'm testifying against him."

Kayla's eyes grew wide. "Against your own father? Was he a bank robber?"

Mitch sighed. "No, not exactly a bank robber. Like I said, it's a long story."

Kayla crossed her arms. "You're not testifying in exchange for – you know, your own deal to stay out of jail?"

Mitch laughed. "I was never going to go to jail, no. Though I guess you could say that no one is completely innocent. When I was younger, like 17 or 18, I wanted to impress my dad and help him with his business. I handled all of the computer stuff for him, and it didn't take long for me to realize that what he was doing was pretty shady. After I left, though, he found new ways to scam even more people. And one day when the FBI came knocking on my door, I knew that I had to give them as much information as I could."

"That's crazy. I can't believe that this is your real life!"

"Me too. And I can never go back to my old life. I'll always be a target."

Kayla took a seat on the couch next to Oliver and played with his ears. "They said that your dad stole billions of dollars?"

"He did."

"How?"

Mitch looked up at the ceiling. "I'm not exactly sure, he did a lot of different things. Insider trading. Dressed up pyramid schemes. He ran a call center that targeted older people, getting them to make bad investments with his company. They drained people's savings, convinced them to cash in their retirement. That kind of thing."

Oliver leaned into Kayla, seemingly fully relaxed. "Wow. What did you do after you stopped working for him?"

Just then, the doorbell rang. Oliver leapt from the couch to bark at the door. Kayla hurried over to reattach Oliver's leash. She dragged him back into the living room, but he was not deterred in his barking.

Mitch opened the front door and welcomed John and Vera Singer into the house. Mitch was grateful that for all of the flaws that his house had, it was at least able to accommodate Vera's wheelchair.

Vera wheeled herself in first, stopping short of Oliver. "Aren't you just the most ferocious little guy?" she said in a high voice.

Oliver immediately stopped barking, his ears perking up. Kayla gave him enough leash to go over and sniff her.

"You're just a little sweetie, yes you are!" Vera continued. Oliver scooted closer to her, almost begging to be petted.

Kayla relaxed his leash a bit more. "I'm sorry about all the barking, I'm still working on his manners."

"Oh that's nothing," said Vera with a smile. "Our last dog was a German Shepherd. He could scare away anyone with his bark."

Kayla smiled and stood up. "It's so nice to finally meet you. My name is Kayla Smith and I heard about what happened to your home. I'm a journalist, and I'd like to help you in any way that I can."

Mitch shot Kayla a look. Did she have to include the journalist part?

John stepped forward and shook her hand. "It's nice to meet you Kayla, I'm John."

Oliver let out a low grumble and Kayla shushed him.

"Oh, you better backup John!" said Vera. "I don't think he likes you!"

John put his hands up as though he was surrendering. "I understand, he has to protect his lady. I feel the same way about my lady."

Mitch smiled. He liked John pretty much the moment that he met him, but little comments like that made his like for him grow even more. Mitch wanted to love someone one day the way John loved Vera – totally and unconditionally.

"How about everyone comes into the living room," said Mitch, "and have something to drink?"

Kayla went into the kitchen with Mitch to help him with making tea and coffee. Oliver anxiously followed Kayla, as was his custom.

"Aren't they just the cutest?" she said in a hushed voice.

Mitch smiled. "They are. I just wanted to check, though," he said, dropping his voice. "You know that you're not a real journalist, right?"

"Listen buddy, I'm just trying to fully commit to this life." Kayla stared at him for a second before a laugh escaped her mouth. "Okay, I know, but I still feel like I could help them. I had to give them some kind of credentials!"

Mitch smiled. She didn't filter what was in her head before it came out of her mouth. It was the opposite of how he lived his life, but somehow it was growing on him. "You're right. I won't say a word."

They returned to the living room and settled in to hear the full story of the day the tornado hit. From the way John told the story, it seemed that they were lucky to escape with their lives. Vera insisted that it wasn't quite so dramatic, though she admitted that the loss was devastating to them both.

"Our house wasn't fancy," she said. "But it was home. And I could get around in my wheelchair without any problems – John widened all the doors for me and put handles wherever I needed them."

"Like I told Mitch," added John, "the insurance company won't pay for hardly anything. So now, we're stuck living off of the good graces of others. We both worked our whole lives, we paid the insurance all those years. It's not that we want something for nothing."

"Of course not!" said Kayla. "This is an outrage!"

"I looked into it from the insurance side," Mitch said, "and unfortunately I don't think that they are going to budge."

John frowned. "I figured as much."

"Forget the insurance company," said Kayla, leaning forward. "I have a better idea. You guys ever heard of a website called GoFundMe?"

Vera and John looked at each other, then back at Kayla. "Can't say that we have. We don't have a computer."

"Well," she said excitedly, "it's a great online community where you can raise money for any cause."

Vera cocked her head to the side. "Why would anyone give money to us? I'm not even sure that I want to ask folks for money."

"You don't have to ask. That's my job," said Kayla. "Listen, I think that you both deserve a safe home. All I'm proposing is that we share your story and anyone who agrees can donate a little bit."

Vera and John looked at each other. This time John spoke. "I don't know about that."

"How is this any different than selling square dance tickets to raise money?" said Kayla. "Except with this, we might actually have the chance to raise enough money to get you back in a suitable home. A home of your own."

For a moment, Mitch wished that he had accepted his dad's money just so he could help these nice people get a safe place to live. He couldn't bring that up at this moment, obviously, so he kept it to himself.

Finally, Vera spoke. "Well, if that's what you do for a living – tell people's stories – and you think that ours is worth telling, I don't see why not."

Kayla squealed with delight. "You won't regret it! If I can show people how lovely both of you are, I'm sure that we'll have no problem raising some money."

John wagged a finger at her. "Now young lady, you won't get anywhere in this world with flattery."

Kayla laughed. "I'm sorry, I won't do it again."

The Singers left after another hour, and after seeing them off, Mitch felt that he needed to ask Kayla some questions.

"Do you really think that you can pull this off?"

Kayla pursed her lips and paused for a moment. "I don't know, honestly. But I have to try."

"That's good enough for me," said Mitch. "You can count me in."

"Great! I need to find a decent camera that we can use for taking pictures and videos."

Mitch nodded. "I can take care of that."

She bit her lip. "And I'll need a decent computer to edit it all together…"

Mitch pointed to the other room. "I have one here. They gave one to me so I can, you know, pretend to sell insurance."

"How's that going for you?" she asked with a smile.

"Just terrific."

She laughed. "Mitch, I think we are going to make a beautiful team."

The thought of working with her thrilled him. "I think you're right."

Chapter 12

Over the next few days, Kayla spent a lot of time with the Singers. She wanted to get a good idea of their history before the square dance so she could complete the fundraising video. That way, she could share the completed website and video with everyone who attended the square dance, and they could help get the word out.

In talking with the Singers, she learned that John was a veteran and worked as a plumber until his back gave out, and Vera worked as a nurse's aide until a car accident left her paralyzed.

"I always wanted to have children," Vera confided. "But we were not so blessed. Do you have any children?"

Kayla shook her head. "No. Hopefully one day."

"Are you married?"

"Nope, not yet," Kayla replied. She felt like she was back in an exam room with one of her patients. Older women were always the most concerned with her love life.

When these comments first started during her training, she would get a bit annoyed. She wanted to say, "Listen! I'm not think-ing about boys! I'm thinking about the best way to treat your diabetes!" But now it never annoyed her; she found their concern sweet. She was starting to get concerned herself, really.

"Do you have your eye on anybody?"

"No," Kayla airily said as George flashed through her mind. "Right now Oliver has my full attention."

Vera was undeterred. "How do you know Mitch? John said that he's pretty good with his hands. He's not bad looking, either."

Kayla suppressed a smile. "We're just friends. If that. To be honest, I don't think he's my biggest fan."

Vera smiled knowingly. "Why not? You're young and smart! And you're so elegantly tall and beautiful."

Kayla laughed. "You're starting to sound like my mother. Though she tells me that I'm too tall for the aggressive personality that I have. She says that I scare the guys away with being as big as they are, and then on top of that, I'm too pushy."

"Pushy is good," said Vera matter of factly. "A woman needs to be pushy to get through this life."

"That's exactly how I see it."

She always blamed her habit of scaring suitors away on being almost six feet tall, but Kayla knew there was more to it than that. She couldn't help being pushy, though. She got a lot of ideas, and she liked to make things happen. Kayla was never one to sit around and wait for someone to help her. And her newest goal was getting the Singers a suitable home.

She made sure to interview some people in town in addition to some of the Singers' friends and family.

All of this traveling and meeting new people was good for Oliver – a challenge, but a good challenge. Naturally, he grumbled and complained whenever a man got too close to him, but overall Kayla was impressed with how well he behaved.

She also worked on putting him in his crate every day with treats so that he learned it was a nice place to be, and not a place that he should start whining and howling as soon as she told him to go inside. He didn't have any more incidents in the cabin, but she still felt awful about the chair that he damaged. She didn't have the heart to tell Isabelle about it yet.

After getting all of the footage that she needed, she spent two full days at Mitch's place to edit the Singers' video and then another day to set up the fundraiser online. As she worked on the computer, Mitch either tinkered around the house, fixing things, or bribed Oliver's affection with treats.

Oliver refused to let Kayla out of his sight; Mitch started calling him "Agent Oliver," joking that he was on special order from the FBI to protect Kayla. For much of the time while she worked, Oliver sat nearby on the floor having a conversation (or argument through dog grumbles) with Mitch.

"Now Ollie, I'd really like to give you this treat, but you will have to come over here and take it from my hand."

Oliver was stubborn. He sat and stared, whimpering and whining as if Mitch was asking him to do something impossible. Though Oliver had grown more comfortable with Mitch, as soon as something was asked of him, he grew suspicious.

It took him ten minutes to get close enough to finally snatch the treat out of Mitch's hand. Once he had it, he felt comfortable enough to let Mitch pet him.

It took so long for Kayla to complete the video and website that by the end, Oliver was even giving Mitch paw on command. Kayla uploaded everything onto the fundraising site, hoping that it would take off on its own.

It didn't.

She was a bit stumped with what to do next.

Mitch had some suggestions. "We could try sending it to some of the nearby news stations?"

"Why didn't I think of that?" Kayla replied with a groan.

Mitch frowned. "You *are* the journalist, I thought you would've thought of that already."

She ignored his sassy comment and sent out twenty emails with a link to the fundraiser. She also posted the video on YouTube, because why not? She knew that they would need some luck for this to catch on, and she planned to find more places to post it that week.

When Kayla got back to her cabin that night, she was wiped out. She considered skipping dinner and eating some trail mix, but right around dinnertime there was a knock at her door.

She opened the door just a crack to see who it was. Oliver was not pleased at all – he stood behind her and barked.

"George!" Kayla said, an excited flutter running through her stomach. "How's it going?"

"You tell me," he said. "We missed you on two trail rides and one river rafting expedition. Did you get sick of us already?"

So he noticed that she wasn't around? And missed her, apparently?

"No, of course not. I've just been spending a lot of time working on a fundraiser for the Singers."

"I'm glad to hear you're dedicated to their cause, because I was hoping you'd want to go to the square dance tomorrow night."

Kayla giggled. Not her coolest moment, but she needed to act like she didn't know about the square dance so he wouldn't realize that she was giggling from excitement. "A real life square dance?"

George laughed. "Yes, a real life square dance. The churches try to have at least one a year. There'll be food, raffles...I think the proceeds this year go to the Singers."

"Then I definitely can't miss it," said Kayla. "Except...I don't know how long Ollie can be left home alone."

"I'm sure he'll be fine. I'll see you there at seven?"

Kayla smiled. Even if she could only go for an hour, she'd make sure it was when George was there. "Sure. See you then."

She closed the door and turned to Oliver. "Listen Buddy, you're going to have to go in your crate tomorrow for a couple of hours. And you can't whine and cry like I'm torturing you by keeping you from eating all of the chairs and all of the bread. Okay?"

He wagged his tail. He could tell that she was asking something of him, he just didn't know what. He ran into the other room to fetch a tennis ball, because that was always a good guess.

The morning before the square dance, Kayla went over to Mitch's place to check if she got any emails back about the fundraiser. Unfortunately, there wasn't a single response.

"Try not to worry yet," said Mitch. "It's Friday, people get backed up with their emails. I think we'll hear something by Monday."

"I hope so," she said.

After that, she took Oliver on a two hour hike. They took a few breaks here and there – Kayla made sure to bring water for them both – and a few times they came upon a nice field for her to throw a tennis ball at Oliver's request.

When Oliver tired of chasing the ball, he hunkered down next to Kayla, rolling over so he laid pressed up against her thigh. She loved feeling his weight cuddled up against her like that; it made her want to sit and pet him for the rest of the day.

When they got back to the cabin, Oliver was exhausted, just as she hoped he'd be. He didn't put up a fight getting into his crate, and he fell asleep almost as soon as he laid his head down. She quietly took a shower and got ready for the dance, and when she was done, he was still sleeping peacefully. Kayla tried her best to quietly close the door to the crate, but he opened his eyes and looked at her.

Caught!

"Listen Ollie, I need to go out for a little bit. But I'll give you a treat and you can just nap until I get back, okay?"

He looked at her, then down at the treat that she slipped into the crate. Instead of eating it, he rested his head on top of it.

That was one of his quirks – he wouldn't eat any treats until she got back home. She wasn't sure if it was some sort of a protest on his part, or if he wanted to save it for the celebration he always threw whenever she came through the door.

Every time she got home, even if she was only gone for ten minutes, he acted like it was the best moment of his life: running around, grabbing toys, rolling onto his back to show his belly. Kayla loved that he did it, and she celebrated too, saying his name in a high pitched voice and telling him what a good boy he was. From the outside, they'd both look like loons. But that was one of the best parts of having a dog – they got to be loons together.

She slipped out of the cabin and stood outside the door for a minute. Satisfied that she didn't hear Ollie whining or barking, she left for the square dance.

The first person she ran into when she got there was Mary, the head of the church fundraising committee. They chatted and Kayla told her about her own attempts to fundraise, and Mary promised to tell everyone about the website.

After Mary took her around to meet other members of the church, Kayla put in for a few raffle tickets and grabbed a bottle of water. She found Isabelle and joined her for some excited chatter.

Kayla kept an eye out for George, but so far he was a no-show. She didn't want to ask Isabelle about him, because she didn't want Isabelle to know that she was looking forward to seeing him.

As it turned out, Isabelle had her eye on a guy herself. "I'm sure he's not as sophisticated as all the guys you meet in New York City, but he's pretty nice."

"You should ask him to dance!" said Kayla, giving her a nudge.

Isabelle shook her head. "I could never do that."

"Come on, of course you could. I bet he's more scared of you than you are of him."

Isabelle smiled. "It doesn't matter, you're not going to get me to go over there asking anyone to dance."

"Suit yourself," Kayla said with a shrug.

"Is that what you do in New York?" asked Isabelle.

Kayla laughed. Poor Isabelle thought that she was some sort of worldly New Yorker, when in truth, she practically lived in the country herself. Isabelle was so fascinated by it all, though.

"To be honest, not really. I spend too much time working to meet any guys."

"You're so confident, though. You can probably just go up to any guy and ask him to dance."

At that moment, Kayla caught sight of George across the room. Her stomach dropped. "Not exactly any guy," Kayla responded.

Before she could motion for George to come over, Mitch stepped into their circle.

"Hi Isabelle, hi Kayla."

Kayla said hello without losing sight of George out of the corner of her eye. She must've missed Mitch earlier since he blended into the sea of cowboy hats.

"Nice hat," she said with a smirk. "I left mine at home."

He sighed. "John made me buy it. Do I look completely ridiculous?"

"No, I'm just messing with you," she said with a laugh. She debated getting a hat of her own, of course, but felt like too much of a phony. In truth, Mitch looked good in his hat. Actually, he looked *really* good.

"Alright," Mitch said, "in that case, would you do me the honor of reserving the next dance for me?"

Isabelle blushed and turned towards Kayla, excitement brimming in her eyes.

Kayla lost sight of George. It seemed like he'd left the room just as quickly as he came in.

"Sure, why not."

Mitch offered his hand and Kayla accepted.

"Let's go cowboy."

She decided that she should stop thinking about how cute Mitch looked in that hat and instead focus on what moves were being called out. They got in place and the music started. It was an upbeat tune and everyone joined hands. Kayla tried to keep from giggling.

They kept up with the group pretty well until they heard, "Swing your partner high and low!"

too attached. Yet at the same time, he couldn't imagine being in Cody without her.

He brought a child-size carton of milk over to Vera and asked her if he could do anything else.

"I'm just fine young man, why don't you ask some of the young ladies to dance?"

He smiled. "I will."

He made his way over to Isabelle and Kayla. Kayla seemed to be trying to convince Isabelle to ask a guy to dance.

"He's not gonna notice you if you just stand here in the corner," argued Kayla.

Isabelle looked absolutely tortured. "You don't know that."

Kayla sighed. "Listen, at least dance with someone else so that he can see you and get a little jealous."

Isabelle frowned. "I don't know."

Mitch offered his hand. "I think my terrible dancing skills could be of use here."

Kayla raised an eyebrow at him. "I didn't expect you to be this enthusiastic of a square dancer."

He shrugged. "Anything in the service of love."

Kayla snorted with laughter and Isabelle took his hand. They made their way to the dance floor to get ready for the next song, one that Isabelle told him was a classic: *She'll be Coming 'Round the Mountain.*

"How are we supposed to dance with this?" asked Mitch.

"You'll see!"

They joined hands with the group and marched in a circle. Then a couple of things happened that Mitch wasn't ready for – when it came time to partner off, he spun the wrong way and found himself lined up with another man from the group. They both laughed it off and tried to catch up with their partners.

In his old life, he would've been too embarrassed to dance in public or do anything that made him uncomfortable. But somehow, Mitch was very different from Jason. He was in a new place with total strangers and surprisingly, he felt more like himself. It made him feel like he had the chance to become the man he wanted to be, and not just a man running from his father's mistakes.

When the song finished, Isabelle shook his hand and gave him a grateful smile. "You're not half bad," she said.

"I'll take it."

She started walking back towards Kayla. Mitch was going to follow until he saw John talking to George. For some reason, it made the hair on the back of his neck stand up. He watched as John followed George out of the room.

Mitch didn't know what compelled him to do this, but he followed them. He did it in a sneaky way. Maybe he was inspired by how cool the FBI agents were in catching his dad, but something inside of him told him that this was the answer to the bad feeling that George gave him. He was able to follow them undetected into the church basement.

To his surprise, there were about fifteen people milling about. John took a seat in the back, and George went to the front of the room. Mitch watched through a crack in the door.

"Thank you all so much for coming here today," said George. "I am so excited to get you involved in this investment opportunity."

Mitch's stomach dropped. All he could see was the back of George's head and the smiling faces of several of the kindly church members. How did George get them all here? And how was it possible that a wrangler would have an "investment opportunity" for them?

Mitch listened to George's impassioned speech, complete with graphs and charts that promised to double the required $3,000 initial investment in six weeks. He was trying to make himself seem like an up-and-coming businessman, talking about some sort of internet venture that he knew these older folks would not question.

He wanted to bust down the door and tell them that they are all about to be scammed, but he resisted. From his dad's many schemes over the years, Mitch knew how George would respond; he'd just find each individual later and convince them that Mitch was some sort of a jealous foe.

Instead, Mitch took out his phone and recorded parts of the presentation. He needed to come up with a plan to debunk whatever George was telling these people.

The presentation wrapped up after about twenty minutes and Mitch made a hasty exit to prevent being seen. He waited upstairs until he saw John and some of the other members of the audience filtering back upstairs.

"John, I need to talk to you," said Mitch.

"Is everything okay?" John put a hand on his shoulder.

"I'm not sure," said Mitch. "Please tell me that you didn't sign any money away to George Walters."

"Not yet," he said. "He won't accept applicants for two weeks, and there's only a limited number he can take. I want to talk to Vera first, of course."

Mitch frowned. "I heard the presentation, it sounds a bit like – well, how about you, me, and Kayla talk it over together later."

John nodded. "Sure, I don't mind if you want to throw your hat in the ring."

That was not Mitch's intention, but at least George didn't take any money yet – it was a clever move for him to say there were a limited amount of spots. Definitely something old Marty would've done.

Mitch turned around to see if he could grab Kayla, but she was talking to George, laughing and fiddling with her hair. He felt a knot in his stomach.

He decided that he needed some fresh air and went outside, taking a seat on a bench. It'd be difficult to convince Kayla that George was up to no good. He needed to get more information. And he needed to protect the Singers, along with all of the other people in this town, until he figured it out.

Mitch went back inside once he gathered his thoughts. He was disappointed to find that Kayla was still chatting with George. For some reason, he couldn't wait a second longer to tell her.

"Kayla, do you have a second? I need to talk to you."

"What's up Mitch?"

He shifted uncomfortably. He didn't know how to get her away from George without telling her some sort of a lie. So he came up with a white lie. "I think I saw a dog running around outside unattended."

Her eyes widened. "Really? Where?"

"Can't handle a little dog by yourself?" asked George with a smirk.

Mitch ignored him. "Out back, I'll show you."

George didn't follow, and when they got outside, Mitch shut the door behind them.

"Where is he?" said Kayla.

"There is no dog, I just needed to talk to you."

Kayla crossed her arms. "Did you just use a dog against me?"

"Listen, this is important. I saw something really weird going on with George."

Kayla stared at him. "What?"

"He had some sort of...presentation going on. Downstairs. I saw John go in there with him, and a bunch of other older folks."

"And?"

Mitch could see that he was losing. "Well, I couldn't hear exactly what was going on, but it seemed a bit shady. I wanted to talk to John about it."

"Don't tell me that you think George is spying on us."

"No, that's not what it seemed like. It just seemed like whatever he was doing, he didn't want anyone to know."

She narrowed her eyes. "Right, which is why he did it at a busy square dance. You automatically assume that he's up to no good?"

"It's not that I assume, it's that –"

Kayla rolled her eyes. "I'm going back to the dance. I don't know what you have against George, but you need to get over it."

She turned and walked back to the building. Mitch felt the frustration rising in his chest. It reminded him of when he was younger and he knew that his dad was up to no good, but he didn't know exactly what.

Except he wasn't a kid anymore. He had resources, he could figure things out. He would find out what George was up to and he would expose him, even if it meant turning Kayla against him.

Maybe it'd be better that way. If she despised him, it'd be easier to say goodbye to her when her time in Cody was done.

George would be of some use after all.

Chapter 14

Without thinking, Kayla stormed back inside to find Isabelle.

"Have you seen George?"

Isabelle turned around. She seemed a bit startled. "No, why?"

Kayla opened her mouth to talk again before realizing why Isabelle seemed a bit off. The guy she liked, Corey, was standing next to her.

"Oh, no reason! I'm actually headed home, I'll see you tomorrow?"

"Sure!" Isabelle replied. "I'll see you then."

Kayla said goodbye to the Singers, and after looking around one last time for George, she headed out to her car. As she drove, she grew a bit nervous about what she might find when she got home. Hopefully, Oliver wasn't able to escape or cause any damage. She learned her lesson to not leave his bed or his bowl of water inside the crate; everything was fair game to be destroyed when he felt anxious.

She opened the front door of the cabin and called out to him. "Ollie, I'm home!"

He whimpered from the other room and she hurriedly made her way back to him. She found him in his crate, with nothing destroyed, and his tail wagging. As soon as she opened the crate door, he ran out, licked her, and bowed into a play pose before running off to grab a toy to drop at her feet.

"Aren't you just a little angel? Yes you are! You are *such* a good boy!"

This went on for the next few minutes – Oliver running and jumping around Kayla as she told him what a good boy he was.

Kayla was truly impressed that he behaved so well while she was gone. Plus, he was the only boy in her life that made any sense. George asked her to go to the dance and after spending five minutes talking to her, he disappeared. He didn't even ask her to dance, not even once!

Mitch showed up in his cowboy hat and was more than willing to dance, which was totally out of character for him. It seemed like he was being nice to her, but then it seemed like he just had a bone to pick with George. What was that even about? Was he jealous?

None of it made any sense. She decided to avoid both of them for the next few days and instead focus on hanging out with Isabelle and Oliver.

It worked until Monday. By then she was anxious to see if she'd gotten any responses about the fundraiser. She couldn't log into email on her phone, because the Marshals made sure it was blocked. That was smart of them – because she'd probably end up getting tracked somehow – but also inconvenient.

In the beginning, she thought it was freeing to not have a computer of her own to waste time on. Now it was annoying. She had to go talk to Mitch anytime she needed to check her email, and it was getting old.

Nevertheless, Monday after lunch she got Oliver in the car and drove over to see Mitch. On the way there, she told herself that she was not going to talk to him about George or anything unrelated to the fundraiser.

She got to his front door and knocked. Oliver was excited. For some reason, he really enjoyed going to other people's homes. He was always more relaxed when visiting others; Kayla thought that it might be because he didn't think of it as his territory, so he didn't have to guard it as fiercely.

She looked down at him, obediently sitting at her side, butt wiggling wildly from his wagging tail, and she felt her heart gush.

"Stop being so stinking cute," she whispered.

He gazed back at her, tongue hanging out of his mouth, eyes full of adoration.

Kayla was surprised when John opened the door. "Hey!" she said.

"Hi Kayla, it's good to see you. Come on in. Mitch was just showing me some of the people who donated to the fundraiser."

She felt her heart leap; what if the whole thing was funded over the weekend?

"We raised some money?"

"You bet we did!" He stepped aside to let her in.

Oliver gave him a sniff before darting away to run up and down the stairs after a tennis ball that Mitch bought for him.

"We raised almost two hundred dollars!"

"Oh," Kayla said, trying to hide her disappointment. That was nice of course, but she wanted to raise enough to get these people a new house. Two hundred dollars would buy them a nice dollhouse, but not much more.

"Hi Kayla," said Mitch. He wasn't wearing his cowboy hat, but he was wearing a distracting shirt. Maybe he'd worn it before and she hadn't noticed. It was a black button down shirt, nothing fancy, but it really suited him. It made his green eyes stand out, and Kayla hated that she noticed that.

"Hey Mitch. Do you mind if I check my email?"

"Of course, go ahead."

She got onto the computer and logged into her email account. She was excited when she saw that she had seven responses to the emails she'd sent out on Friday.

The first six were rejections – they all thanked her for the information, but said they couldn't run the story. No room in the schedule, they all claimed.

"What do they mean they don't have room for it?" she said. "What else are they covering? This is local news – well, it's fairly local. All within a three hour radius. This is a real story! They run stories all the time that aren't even related to the people living here. And who tells them to do that, some executive? Are they just broadcasting whatever some rich guy in a suit tells them to broadcast?"

"Unfortunately, a lot of us spend most of our time doing what rich guys in suits tell us to do," Mitch commented.

She shot him a dirty look. "What's that supposed to mean?"

He put his hands up. "Nothing! I was agreeing with you."

John walked into the room and Kayla felt her anger subsiding. She opened the last email. The first line said, "Thank you for sharing this amazing story. We would love to feature this next week on our evening programming."

She let out a squeal.

John leaned in to look at the screen. "Did you get some good news?"

"Yes! The station over in Jackson Hole is going to run your story!"

John's eyes grew wide. "Really? We're going to be on the news?"

Kayla grabbed his hands and nodded excitedly. "Yes!"

"I need to call Vera," said John. "Mitch – do you have a phone that I can use?"

Mitch pulled out his cell phone. "Sure, take your time."

John left the room, leaving them alone. Kayla was determined to not say anything. She turned around to read the email again.

Mitch, for once, broke the silence. "That's amazing Kayla. What you've done is – well, I'm just so impressed."

Kayla's grudge was quickly fading. She turned around to see Mitch standing there, a sincere look in his eyes.

"Thanks Mitch."

John came back into the room. "She didn't have much time to talk, but she was very excited when I told her. And she's very impressed with the two hundred dollars that you've already raised! That might be enough for us to get to the investment minimum."

Kayla tilted her head to the side. "What investment minimum?"

John handed the cell phone back to Mitch. "Well George was telling us – if we could bring three thousand dollars to the table, he has a company that we can invest in so we could double the money in just a few weeks."

Kayla shot Mitch an uneasy look. "Really? That seems a bit too good to be true."

John shrugged. "It might be. I planned to talk to Mitch about it today."

"Well," Mitch said, crossing his arms, "I would say hold off on that for now. I want to look into it."

John nodded. "That's good enough for me. I better get going, we have some friends coming over and Vera needs some help getting everything ready."

He gave Kayla a hug before he left, thanking her again for all that she was doing for them. A little pang of panic ran through her – she still hadn't raised very much money. Luckily, the worry of disappointing them was enough to spark some new ideas.

After he left, Kayla announced that she and Oliver had to get going, but Mitch said he had something he wanted to show her first. She followed him out to the garage, Oliver gleefully bounding behind her.

It was an organized space, with tools neatly hanging on a pegboard against the wall. There was wood dust on all of the counters, and several projects seemed to be in progress. Mitch ducked down to grab something and handed it to her.

"Oh my gosh," she said. "Is this what I think it is?"

He nodded. "Yep. Oliver and I worked together to get you a replacement chair leg."

She couldn't believe it. "How is that possible? He chewed off so many pieces of it. This looks brand new."

"That's because it is. I ordered a piece of wood that I thought would match, and then I fashioned a new leg based off of the old one. I can come over whenever you have some time and reattach it. I don't think anyone will be able to tell the difference."

Awed, she turned it over in her hand. "It's amazing. Thank you so much. I felt so bad and have been avoiding telling Isabelle about what happened."

Oliver sat at her feet, looking up expectantly at the chair leg.

"Oh no you don't," she wagged a finger at him. "This one is off limits."

Mitch laughed. "Just let me know if he gets a taste for any other wood furniture, and I'll be happy to replace it for you."

Now it was *really* hard to be mad at him. She cleared her throat. "Thank you so much, Mitch. This is awesome."

"You're very welcome."

Oh, what the heck. "I was going to take Oliver on a walk – well, more of a hike. Would you want to come?"

He looked surprised. "Sure, that'd be nice. You're saving me from learning about whole life insurance."

Kayla made a face. "Sounds like torture. Let's go!"

She gave him a ride back to the ranch; she preferred hiking around there because the trails were clearly defined and she felt like she knew where she was going. She waited until they were about a mile into the hike before bringing up an awkward topic. "So this investment opportunity that John mentioned?"

Mitch nodded his acknowledgment.

She continued. "This is the one that you heard George talking about at the dance?"

"It was. I didn't hear the whole thing, but from what I heard... let's just say that it sounded like one of my dad's old schemes. He said that they would need to recruit at least five more people after they enrolled."

Kayla groaned. "You think it was a pyramid scheme?"

"I'm not sure," Mitch said with a sigh. "I don't have enough evidence yet to know what was really going on, but it doesn't look good."

Kayla nodded. "That's fair. I just can't believe that George would do something so stupid. Like, I think if he is involved, he must just not understand."

Mitch was silent for a beat. "Yeah, maybe."

"So you really weren't involved in any of your dad's scams?"

"No," Mitch said, looking straight ahead. "Like I said, when I was younger, I wanted to impress my dad. He wanted me to go to law school so I could be his lawyer. That didn't work out, luckily, and by that time I understood that he was a criminal. I knew a lot of his associates, still, because I did all of his record keeping for a little while. But that was as deep as I ever went."

"Oh, I see."

Mitch turned towards her. "I promise that I am not a criminal. I'm a carpenter. Or at least, I was."

Kayla smiled. "That explains the chair leg."

Mitch laughed. "Yeah. I really miss woodworking. The Marshals said that it would be too suspicious if I picked it up again."

"So you just lose that forever?"

He sighed. "Pretty much."

"Did your dad choke on those french fries because you told him that you were going to tattle on him?"

Oliver dropped his ball at Mitch's feet and then looked at him expectantly. Mitch bent over, grabbed the ball, and threw it far. Oliver took off like a rocket.

"No. I mean, I did tell him that day that I would be testifying against him. But he said that he knew, and that he wasn't angry with me at all."

"Wow," said Kayla. "So he's just really bad at eating french fries."

Mitch laughed. "Not exactly. He choked on his french fries because of something else."

Kayla looked at him. "What?"

He seemed to search her eyes for a moment. "I can't believe I'm telling you this. I haven't told anyone."

Finally, something juicy! "C'mon, I won't tell anyone."

Mitch smiled. "He choked when I told him that I wouldn't take his money."

"Was he trying to pay you off?"

Mitch shook his head. "No, nothing like that. He just felt really bad about – well everything, I guess. And he said that the whole reason that he wanted to make money in the first place was so that I could have a good life. That he just got lost along the way. But he still wanted me to have all the money that he made. Er – stole. And actually, not all of it, the FBI did freeze some of it."

Now Kayla's interest was piqued. "Like how much? Ten thousand? Twenty thousand?"

"That they froze?" Mitch asked.

"No, that he wanted to give you."

Mitch rubbed the back of his neck and turned to look at Oliver, who was rolling in a patch of grass ten feet away. "A lot."

"You can't hold out on me now!" This was fun. Mitch was finally opening up to her. She felt like she hardly knew the man until recently.

"It's just – I haven't talked to *anyone* about this before."

Kayla playfully poked him in the shoulder. "I'm not going to tell anyone. And besides, you don't want the money anyway, right?"

Mitch smiled at her, then looked back out at Oliver. He mumbled something that Kayla couldn't quite hear.

She leaned towards him. "Did you say two *million?*"

"No," he said, looking behind them as though to double check no one was there.

"Oh good, I was about to die. That would be *insane.*"

He cleared his throat. "I said two billion."

Kayla's jaw dropped open. For once, she was at a loss for words. She hadn't noticed that Oliver was standing in front of her, patiently waiting for her to notice that he dropped his ball between her feet. Looking at him made her feel dizzy, so she sat down.

"Are you okay?" Mitch rushed to gently grab her arm, thinking that she was falling.

"I'm fine, I just needed to take a seat."

Oliver playfully nosed the ball towards her. She absentmindedly picked it up and rolled it a few feet away. Oliver gleefully took off after it.

Mitch sat down next to her. "Really, are you feeling okay? I'm sorry, I didn't mean to shock you with that."

She waved a hand. "No, *I'm* sorry, I've never met a billionaire before and I'm just having a hard time wrapping my head around that number."

He laughed. "I'm not a billionaire. Like I told my dad, I'm not taking any of that money."

"Why not?" sputtered Kayla. "I mean – he said it was for you."

"Yeah, and it was stolen from hard working people. I don't want it. I have no need for it."

He got up and wrestled the ball away from Oliver. She watched him for a few minutes, trying to absorb what she'd just heard.

It wasn't just the money that shocked her – she'd assumed all along that he was rich from whatever crimes he'd committed to get into witness protection. But she never imagined he was *that* rich.

Or that he was so...moral. And that he'd never committed a crime at all. She'd written him off after he insulted her; he'd made assumptions about her intelligence and she made assumptions about his character.

And now...now she didn't know what to think.

Chapter 15

Oliver ran over to Mitch, taunting him with the tennis ball. Every time that Mitch went to grab it, Oliver would run off triumphantly. After this happened two or three times, Kayla reappeared.

"I think he's done playing by the rules of fetch," she said.

"I think you're right."

Kayla turned to him. "So am I allowed to ask you any more questions about this billion dollars that you don't want, or is that off-limits?"

He knew that he should never have mentioned it. He didn't know what got into him. It wasn't that he was bragging or anything; he found it all quite embarrassing. But he felt like if there was anyone in the world that he could trust with this information, it was Kayla. It felt freeing to get it out in the open.

"It's not off-limits," he replied. "There's just nothing else to say about it."

She crossed her arms. "Well, I've been thinking about it, and I have some things to say."

Mitch resisted smiling. He didn't want to encourage her. "Oh really?"

"I had a hard time understanding what that number means. Two *billion*. I had to wrap my head around it."

"Uh huh."

"A billion is one thousand millions, right?"

Mitch had to think for a moment. "Yeah, it is."

"Okay." Kayla clapped her hands together. "That means you could pick one *thousand* charities and give them each one *million* dollars, and you would still have the other *billion* dollars left over."

He knew where she was going with this, and he did not want to have this discussion. "Yeah, except that money is not mine and I'm never going to accept it. So I have zero billion dollars."

"But you could accept it! You could do so much good with it."

Mitch shook his head. How could she ever understand? How would she ever know how much hurt and shame his father brought into the world to get that money?

"It's not that simple. I wish I could explain it to you, but I can't."

She stared at him, jaw clenched. "I wish that I could explain to you what a waste it is. What's going to happen to all of that money? Is it just going to end up in some government fund?"

"What do you have against the government?" he said with a laugh, trying to lighten the mood.

Kayla wasn't having it. "Nothing. But do you really believe whatever random thing happens to seized money would be better than what you could do with it?"

He covered his eyes with his hand. "I don't know, Kayla. I've always been running from my dad and his schemes and his money. I didn't want it before, and I don't want it now. I just want to have my own life."

"As an insurance salesman?"

He shrugged. "Yeah, if that's normal. That's what I want."

Kayla stared at him, and he was afraid that she might start yelling. Instead, she called Oliver over and reattached his leash. "Alright Ollie, you look pretty tired. Let's get you back home."

They didn't have far to walk back to the ranch; Kayla didn't mention another word about the money. Mitch was relieved because he didn't know what else to say. When he first told her about it, a small part of him hoped that she would agree with him about not taking it. That was foolish.

Kayla offered to drive him back home, but first he wanted to reattach the chair leg. It only took him about ten minutes, and then she drove him back to his house.

The whole time she chatted pleasantly about ideas that she had for the fundraiser and how exciting it was that a news station agreed to cover the story. Mitch agreed with her and thought she did excellent work on the whole thing. He was cautiously optimistic about the fundraiser's success at first, but more and more he was impressed by how skilled and dedicated Kayla was.

They made plans to meet again in a few days to do a tour of Yellowstone National Park. Kayla said that she'd been dying to go ever since she arrived in Cody. Mitch also wanted to go, but in a more abstract way. Knowing that he would be living in Cody for the rest of his life, he didn't feel as much of a rush to do things. He knew that was silly and that he should seize the day, so he was glad that Kayla was always thinking ahead and planning experiences.

Though he managed to make some new friends at the square dance, he didn't have any other social events planned until the trip with Kayla. He was forced to focus on his insurance work. He got through all the training and was technically supposed to start selling insurance. It was time for him to start taking phone calls for people who had questions and needed a local consult.

He still hadn't signed up for any shifts, though, and since he worked on commission, this would soon become a problem.

He decided that there was one thing that he needed to do before he fully committed to his new career: find the truth about George.

He spent almost a full day looking into George's past. Although he knew a guy through his dad who could do it much more quickly, he was unable to contact him. The Marshals were clear that he could not contact anyone that he used to know for any reason.

After a bit of internet detective work, though, Mitch was able to trace a few of the ranches where George worked over the past few years. Mitch made calls and sent emails; he even had a picture of George from the New Morning Ranch website to send along with his inquiries.

When it was time for his trip to Yellowstone with Kayla, all but one of the ranches responded with information. He wasn't surprised by what he found, but he was worried how Kayla would take the news.

He drove to pick her up at the ranch early that morning.

"What? No Oliver today?" he asked as she hopped into his truck.

"No," she sighed. "But luckily Isabelle said that she could check in on him today, so I have a dog sitter. I don't have to worry about him; I think Yellowstone would be a bit dangerous for him."

"I don't think he'd appreciate the other tourists," said Mitch.

"Definitely not."

Mitch gave her an update about the fundraiser. Although she was disappointed that they hadn't made much progress, she was hopeful that the spot on the local news would change things. "This may be all it takes to get national attention for our cause."

He weighed his next words carefully. "I don't mean this in a bad way, but what if it doesn't?"

Kayla sighed. "I know what you mean, I'm not offended. If that's the case, I'm prepared for it. I have six more ideas that we can try."

Mitch smiled. She definitely wasn't someone who gave up easily. As much as he admired that, it made what he was about to tell her that much more difficult.

"I've got something to show you," he said. "There's a folder in the glove box that I want you to look through."

"Oh," she said, opening the glove box. "A secret folder, how exciting! Is it going to self-destruct when I'm done with it?"

"No, it won't." Mitch realized he was holding his breath. Exciting wasn't the word he would've used. He was half afraid that once she saw what was inside, she'd tell him to turn around. Or that she'd demand to get out of the car.

She flipped through the pages, reading quietly. Her hand darted to cover her mouth, but still she said nothing. Mitch waited anxiously, his eyes darting between her and the road ahead of them.

After about five minutes, she finally spoke. "It's all true? George has scammed people all over the country?"

Mitch nodded. "It is. I'm sorry."

"Don't be sorry! What are we going to do about this? He's been traveling around the country and getting away with pyramid schemes for years!"

Mitch felt a weight lift off of his chest. She wasn't angry!

"I know," he said, "it's awful. It seems like he targets older folks, too. And even after he left some of the locations, he convinced people to wire him money. Some people lost their entire savings."

"He told me that he traveled to experience the world! That snake! Look at all of these stories!"

"I know. Once the police catch on, he skips town."

Kayla whipped her phone out of her pocket. "This is unbelievable! I'm calling Isabelle right now."

"Wait," said Mitch. "If you do that and they kick him out, he's just going to get away with it again and start over in some new town."

Kayla sighed. "I guess you're right, but what else are we supposed to do?"

Mitch smiled. "I'm glad to see that you're on board, because that's going to make it much easier."

"Oh," Kayla replied, eyes lighting up, "can we, like, steal his car or something?"

"What?" Mitch laughed. "If we steal his – no, that's not what I was thinking. More like we could pass along a little tip to the FBI. He is a wanted man, after all."

Kayla got so excited that she struck him in the shoulder. "Genius!"

He let out a sarcastic "ow."

"Eek, I'm sorry!" She gingerly rubbed the spot that she just smacked. "I didn't mean to do that."

"It's all right. Do you want to give Agent Simmons a call before we get to Yellowstone?"

Kayla solemnly put her hand over her heart. "I would be honored."

Mitch kept his eyes on the road. He was relieved that she didn't try to defend George. The evidence was pretty clear, but Mitch didn't know how deep Kayla's friendship with George actually went. He could tell that she had a bit of a crush on him. Clearly, though, whatever she felt for him was not enough to make her defend his terrible actions.

It seemed that his luck was turning around, but he reminded himself that he couldn't get too attached to her. The trial was only a few short weeks away, and after that, Kayla would be out of his life forever.

Yet somehow, despite knowing this to be a fact, he found it impossible to stay away from her. It seemed that she had him fully ensnared in her charms.

For once in his life, he decided not to worry about every little thing, and instead enjoy his friendship with this extraordinary woman while it lasted.

Chapter 16

Their trip to Yellowstone was amazing. Kayla felt like she was on an alien planet; everything looked so strange and beautiful.

Exploring the park left her drained, though. That night, she only had the strength to take Oliver on a walk, feed him his dinner, and go to bed. When she awoke the next morning, her entire body felt sore. All this time she thought that she was getting pretty fit by taking Oliver for long walks and hikes, but apparently it was no match for running around Yellowstone Park for a day.

Despite her soreness, Kayla was on a mission. She could not believe that Mitch had access to billions of dollars and thought it was better to leave it lying around to be seized! It's not like she was telling him to accept the money and buy a jet or a private island. Though who was she kidding? He could probably buy a small country with that money.

All she needed him to understand was that he could do so much good with it and potentially undo some of the damage that his father inflicted on the world. He could donate millions upon millions of dollars to charities, or even start his own charity. This money could help people for years after both he and his father were long gone. Kayla planned to tell this to him when she went over later to watch the news broadcast about the Singers.

Despite being dedicated to her mission, there were a few things that she had to do first. After getting up and taking Oliver for a walk, she met up with Isabelle to help her with the horses – something she'd promised to do ages ago when she heard that Isabelle would be short handed for the day.

She was glad that she didn't forget, because Isabelle was all aflutter with news of going to the movies with her crush Corey. Kayla pressed for details, but Isabelle was a bit shy.

"I'm sure it all sounds lame to you," bemoaned Isabelle.

"What? Why would you say that?"

Isabelle sighed. "I just can't imagine how different everything is for you in the city. I'm sure that these all seem like little girl problems."

Kayla laughed as she lifted a saddle from a pony. "You'd be surprised how lame my life is. I haven't gone to the movies with a guy in years. Actually, I haven't gone *anywhere* with a guy in ages."

Isabelle gave her a mischievous smile.

"What's that supposed to mean?" asked Kayla.

Isabelle shrugged. "I mean, you were out with Mitch all day yesterday. I would say that he definitely counts as a guy. A pretty cute guy."

Kayla rolled her eyes. "Believe me, he did not think that it was a date. And neither did I. We are just two people exploring one of this nation's amazing national parks."

"You sound like a brochure," Isabelle shouted from the back of the barn.

"That's what I'm doing here, isn't it? Turning myself into a brochure!"

Kayla wolfed down lunch as quickly as she could before taking Oliver for a nice long walk to tire him out; she needed to carry out the next part of her mission in peace. It worked like a charm, and he went right to his crate and settled in for a nap. She gave him a treat and told him to be a good boy while she was away. Luckily for her, his good boy incidents now far outweighed his naughty incidents. The crate was a huge help, and he didn't seem to mind it now that he understood there was no negotiation about going inside.

She had to go to the library to use a computer, because she didn't want Mitch to see that she was going to search "Marty Brash" online. Also, she wondered if searching Marty's name would trigger some sort of alert and the bad guys would immediately know where she was. That seemed like something out of the movies, though, and she figured that she couldn't be the only person in the country to know the man's name.

After about two hours of research, she learned more about the crimes that Marty orchestrated. Most exciting to her were the online support groups formed by people who lost their pensions or were scammed out of money in some other way. The ones nearby weren't directly related to Marty, but they were close enough.

This was exactly what Mitch needed to see: the impact of these scams on real people. She printed a few things out before rushing back to the cabin to pick up Oliver.

She made it to Mitch's place just in time. John and Vera were already there, and Mitch made several bowls of popcorn for everyone to enjoy.

"I would've gone with buffalo chicken dip for this sort of party myself," she told him as she accepted a small bowl of popcorn. "But this is nice too."

He gave her a smile that told her he wasn't going to take the bait of arguing with her. "I wouldn't want to subject these nice people to my terrible cooking."

Kayla had never been so excited to watch the news. First, there was a story about some burglaries in Jackson Hole. Next was something about a mountain lion – it didn't catch Kayla's interest – and then a story about the price of a school lunch. Finally, towards the end, a glorious five minute spot aired that was dedicated entirely to the Singers.

It mainly highlighted footage of the aftermath of the tornado and fundraiser that Kayla set up. The last shot was of John and Vera holding hands as they gazed onto the field where their home used to be.

"It's hard to believe it's all gone," said John to the reporter. "But people like our friend Kayla really give us hope."

A hot feeling ran through Kayla's body. To her horror, a picture of her from the square dance appeared on screen. She couldn't hear what was being said on the program because her mind was in such a panic.

"There you are," chimed a voice in her head. "You and your dumb non-witness protected face plastered over hundreds, if not thousands, of TVs at this second."

The story ended. Kayla sat there stunned. She didn't want to look at Mitch. He was probably shooting daggers with his eyes.

"I think that was lovely!" Vera said excitedly.

John nodded encouragingly. "And I hope you don't mind that we snuck in some credit to you."

"No, no," she said a little too forcefully. "I'm just...a bit camera shy."

Vera had a puzzled look on her face. "But you're a journalist!"

"I am, I just prefer to stay behind the scenes," replied Kayla. She cautioned a look at Mitch. His expression was stony and unreadable.

John and Vera thanked her again for all of her help and reminded her that even if the fundraiser didn't work, they appreciated her efforts all the same. Kayla hugged them both and said goodbye.

After they left, Kayla knew she had to face Mitch. She found it extremely hard to do so, but there was nowhere to hide.

He broke the silence. "I think that whole segment was amazing."

"Yeah," she scoffed, "except that my stupid face was broadcast all over the news!"

He flinched. "You don't have a stupid face. And yeah, that wasn't ideal. But hopefully the guys looking for us don't watch Jackson Hole's local news every night."

Kayla groaned. "They probably do. They're probably coming here right now."

"I don't think it's *that* bad," Mitch said with a laugh. "We should let Perez know what happened so –"

Kayla cut him off. "No. They told me not to attract attention to myself, and being on the news is the exact opposite of keeping a low profile. They're going to kick me out!"

"They're not going to kick you out," Mitch said evenly. "I won't let them. I'll refuse to testify."

Kayla felt a breath catch in her throat. Was he serious? He looked serious. But Mitch almost always looked serious because he had resting scowl face.

She cleared her throat. "That's not necessary."

He took a step towards her. "It is. Without me, this is all a waste. I think we should tell them so they can be on the alert for any threats. And if they kick you out, I go too."

Kayla didn't know what to say to that, so her brain offered a lame joke. "Then you'll need your dad's money to hire around the clock protection with retired Navy Seals or something."

He shrugged. "So be it."

Kayla swallowed. Yeah. He was definitely serious. She didn't know what to say. In the silence, she heard a faint sound. "Do you hear that?" she asked.

Mitch turned his head to listen. "I think it's coming from the kitchen."

They walked to the kitchen to find Oliver, triumphantly wagging his tail, tongue hanging out of his mouth as if to say, "Hey guys!" A piece of laminate flooring at least two feet long was detached from the floor. It looked like he dug at it before tugging the corner with his mouth.

Kayla slapped a hand to her forehead. "Oh no, Ollie! I shouldn't have left you unsupervised for so long! What is this!"

Oliver's tail slowly drifted downwards. He dropped his eyes to avoid Kayla's glare.

She turned to Mitch. "I am so sorry, I will replace this!"

But Mitch was already down on his hands and knees, petting Oliver on the back. "That's alright, Ollie! I wanted to pull that up myself anyway. Good job buddy!"

Oliver's tail perked back up and he promptly flipped over, launching his paws into the air and exposing his belly for rubs.

"I really am sorry," Kayla said.

Mitch turned to face her while still rubbing Oliver's belly. "It's really not a problem, the floor is total junk. Plus, we came in after he was done doing it, so even though he knew we were unhappy, he didn't know why. There's no point in shaming him now." He turned back to Oliver. "He's still *a really good boy!*"

Kayla didn't know what was happening, but as she watched burly, lumberjack Mitch on the floor, comforting Oliver in a high pitched voice, something in her heart stirred.

Chapter 17

After Mitch helped Kayla craft a carefully worded email to Perez, Kayla took Oliver, got into her car, and went back to the ranch.

Mitch's place was quiet at night, and while he liked the peace, he also liked having guests around. He didn't mind at all about the damage to the kitchen floor. In fact, it gave him an excuse to replace the floor himself instead of waiting for the landlord to do it.

Mitch was more worried about Kayla being on the news than he let on. It didn't seem like it would be helpful for him to freak out, though, so he kept it to himself.

None of the Marshals contacted him recently with any news about Colin. It'd be surprising if Colin were sharp enough to catch a slip up on the Jackson Hole evening news, but who knows? He could get lucky. It wasn't worth risking Kayla's safety to test Colin Cragin's cleverness.

The next few days were going to be boring for Mitch. He finally signed up for some shifts as an insurance salesman. Though he didn't feel completely comfortable with all of the aspects of it, and he didn't want to give anyone bad advice, he felt like it was now or never. Soon Kayla would go back to Albany and he would have nothing to fill his time.

Sure, he'd made some friends, and he'd found little projects to distract him – like the deal he got on some wood that he used to craft a nice little table. It took hours to complete, and the whole time he knew he should've been working his real job, but it was hard to commit to the transition.

Perez responded to his email two hours after he sent it. She thanked him for making them aware of the news incident, and though they were too late to stop it, they had yet to see any suspicious activity. Mitch had the urge to call her and ask about Colin, but he decided to use Kayla's approach and assume that if there was a problem, they would tell them. He sent Kayla a text message letting her know that he got an email that she shouldn't be worried.

Mitch then dedicated himself to attempting to sell insurance. He managed to sell a few policies, but only because the people who called him knew exactly what they wanted. He started wondering how hard it was going to be to make his living this way. Perhaps the Marshals would allow him a slight career change. Maybe to be a plumber or something – anything other than sitting in front of this computer all day.

When Kayla asked him to take a ride with her after two days of working on insurance, he was more than willing. She could've asked him to shovel horse manure out of the stables for all he cared – anything to take a break. It didn't hurt that it was Kayla asking, either.

For some reason, she insisted on picking him up and being the driver. He had the fleeting thought that her insistence was a bit odd, but he didn't dwell on it.

An hour into their drive, he realized that he should've explored that feeling further. "I didn't think we were going this far from Cody," he said nervously.

Kayla, driving with one hand barely on the wheel, dismissed his concerns. "Listen, we couldn't be going to a safer place."

He raised an eyebrow. "What's that supposed to mean?"

"Don't worry about it."

He wasn't going to give up that easily. "Can I have a hint?"

She bit her lip. "I just wanted to go to a fundraiser."

"Another one? Is it for the Singers?"

"Not exactly..." Her voice trailed off.

Now Mitch was sure that she was hiding something. "Why do I have a bad feeling about this?"

Kayla shrugged. "Who knows! Enjoy the ride!"

Ten minutes later, they arrived at a fire hall. Mitch argued that they shouldn't go inside; what if the people inside saw Kayla's face all over the news? It seemed unwise to go barging into new places.

Kayla wasn't having it. "Oh come on, we can just sit in the back and observe. I promise we won't talk to anyone."

He sighed. "When have you ever *not* talked to people?"

"All right, I guess I'm on my own!" She jumped from the car and walked into the fire hall without him.

He couldn't let her walk in there by herself, so he followed her, accepting a brochure at the door before taking a seat next to Kayla in the very last row.

"If we see anything funny," he said in a whisper, "we're leaving. Okay?"

She nodded solemnly. "Of course."

A man took the podium and introduced himself as the police chief.

"I would like to personally thank you all for being here today. Our town has always stepped up to support one another, and this is no different."

He was met with applause.

Mitch looked at Kayla. She was clapping too. Was this another one of her journalist schemes? She was really enjoying that title to the fullest.

The police chief continued. "As hard as it's been for us to watch our friends and family members be ripped apart by their financial trouble, I'm confident that with all of the great minds we have here today, we will be able to find a solution."

Mitch opened the brochure, looking for a hint of what this was about. It offered no clues. He shot Kayla a look, but she appeared determined to keep staring straight ahead. At this point, people from the crowd got up to tell their stories. They ranged from the very young to the very old, and everyone in between.

From what Mitch could gather, a business set up shop in this town offering advice on financial investments. The salesman provided payday loans as well as tips on how to invest in the stock market. He had glossy magazines with pictures of beautiful time-shares, too. The shop also sold expensive foods that were supposed to help with weight loss.

Mitch leaned into Kayla to quietly say, "It sounds like this was a one stop shop for being scammed."

Kayla nodded. "It's really stunning how aggressive the whole campaign was. From what I read online, and from what we're hearing today, it sounds like hundreds of people lost their savings."

Mitch rubbed his forehead. "Yeah, I'm not surprised. Once he gained their trust it was probably easy."

"Yep," Kayla said quietly. "That's how it seems. Then the guy closed up shop, took all of their investments, sold their debt to collections companies, and left town. Probably to hit the next town over."

Mitch frowned. "Tale as old as time."

He knew what she was doing. Though this wasn't one of his father's schemes – it was a bit too unsophisticated for Marty's recent criminal life – it was a shocking example of how much damage one person could do.

Kayla wanted him to see the human effects of his dad's schemes. But he knew what the effect was, he'd seen it for years. He knew it was devastating. He knew it destroyed families. His dad was a bad guy who did bad things. It was overwhelming to see the harm and chaos that his father caused over the years. That's why Mitch spent so many years running away from it.

"I think we better get going," said Mitch after listening for an hour.

Kayla crossed her arms. "Why? They're just getting started."

"You've made your point," he said. "Let's get out of here before someone sees you."

He watched her face as she clearly debated if she was going to worry about that. "All right," she finally said, "let's go."

Once they were back on the road, Kayla started her campaign again. "Isn't it just amazing, though? How these communities band together?"

Mitch stared out of the window. "It is. I wish them all the best."

Kayla sighed, exasperated. "You know you could help them, right?"

"How? By doing fundraising with them?"

"Ugh!" exclaimed Kayla. "I'm trying to be subtle here, but you're making it really hard."

"There's nothing subtle about it, I know what you want me to do."

Kayla looked at him with narrowed eyes. "Okay? Then what's your argument against it?"

He shook his head. "It's out of the question. There's nothing to discuss. I'm not going to accept my dad's money, not for any reason."

"Even to help all of those people? Don't do it for yourself, do it for them."

"It's not that simple Kayla. There's a lot of – history. And stuff. I'll always be linked to him."

Kayla took her hand off the steering wheel and waved it wildly in the air. "No you wouldn't! You could stay anonymous. No one needs to know."

"Of course they would," he said.

She let out a huff. "Fine. If you refuse to talk about it, we can just ride back in silence."

Mitch sighed. This wasn't how he imagined his evening with Kayla going. Yet there they were.

She was stubborn – extremely stubborn. But she didn't understand that this wasn't her fight. She wouldn't be able to convince him that accepting all that money would bring any more good into the world. Mitch didn't want any part of it.

They drove for the next hour in silence, just as Kayla promised. When she pulled up to his house, he turned to her and felt like he had to say something.

"I'm sorry I disappointed you. I know that it doesn't make sense to you. And I'm sorry."

Kayla looked at him, her lips pressed in a thin line. "Goodnight Mitch."

She wasn't going to budge.

"Goodnight Kayla."

He got out of the car, closed the door, and watched her drive off into the night.

Chapter 18

What a nerve he had. He'd rather not talk to her at all than talk about the billions of dollars he planned to waste? Fine!

Kayla drove home in a huff. How could he be so heartless? Those people weren't directly affected by one of his dad's schemes, but they may as well have been.

None of it mattered to Mitch, though. He didn't want to help them – he didn't want to help anyone because he was a selfish person, just like his father. Kayla couldn't believe that she almost thought he was a nice guy. He *clearly* wasn't.

She was so preoccupied that it felt like she got back to the ranch in no time. Oliver was thrilled to see her, and when she took him on a short walk around the ranch, she ran into Isabelle.

"Hey Kayla, hey Oliver. How's it going?"

"Oh pretty good," Kayla responded. She'd managed to calm down a bit and felt better after walking around. "How're you doing?"

"Great! I was just about to watch the new episode of *Cowboy Looking for Love in the City*."

Kayla suppressed a laugh. "Is that a real show?"

Isabelle beamed. "I know it sounds dumb, but it's cute. Would you want to watch with me? It's online so we can watch anytime."

"I don't have internet access in my cabin," said Kayla.

Isabelle cocked her head to the side. "Yes you do. Every cabin has Wi-Fi and a private password. It would've all been in your welcome instructions."

Kayla covered her eyes. "You have got to be kidding me. I've been going over to Mitch's place for weeks because I didn't think that I had access to the internet, and my phone only barely works here."

Isabelle giggled. "You should've asked. So do you want to watch some cowboys or what?"

Kayla sighed. She couldn't believe that she'd been there for so long and had no idea about the internet. "Sure, that sounds nice. Oliver's been stuck at home all night, and I'm sure he'd love the company."

They headed back to Kayla's cabin. After popping some popcorn, they settled onto the couch next to Oliver.

Kayla was excited to have internet access and connected her phone to it right away. Her fight with Mitch made her feel crabby and homesick. It wouldn't be long before she could return home, and for some reason, she really missed her regular boring life right at that moment.

She was tempted to look at some of the Facebook profiles of her friends and family; it might help her feel less alone. She couldn't log into her account, of course, in case there was some sort of tracker on it. But what harm was there in looking?

Kayla tilted her phone out of Isabelle's view – luckily Isabelle was pretty engrossed in the show. First, Kayla tried to pull up her best friend's page; unfortunately, it was set to private and she couldn't see anything. Almost all of her friends had private accounts. There was only one person she knew who had a public profile for sure, and that was her mom.

After typing in her mom's name, she was able to easily find her and open her profile. Her mom's picture was still the same as it'd been for the past two years, which was oddly comforting for some reason. Kayla scrolled down the page and saw a bunch of activity. Her heart dropped in the pit of her stomach.

"So sorry to hear, best of luck."

"Sending prayers, love you both."

"We made your signature tortellini salad today," wrote Kayla's great aunt. "Get well soon."

Normally Kayla would laugh at a comment like that, so seemingly out of place. But right now she didn't find any of it funny. What happened? Did someone hurt her mom? Or her dad? What was going on?

She scrolled down her mom's Facebook page and was able to figure out that yes, something did happen, and her mom appeared to be in the hospital.

"I need to get home right away," Kayla said out loud.

Isabelle turned to her, alarmed. "Is everything okay?"

"No," she stood, feeling frantic. "I mean, I don't know. It looks like my mom is in the hospital, but I don't know what's going on."

"Can you call her?"

Kayla almost had to bite her tongue to keep from telling Isabelle the truth. "No, I haven't heard from her and – I just need to go home."

Isabelle stood up from the couch, bumping Oliver, who let out an exaggerated sigh. "It's probably too late to fly out tonight, but the first flight usually leaves Cody at 5:30 in the morning. You could catch a flight to Denver and then get back to New York City?"

"Right." Kayla felt like her brain wasn't working. Her mom was hurt. Or sick? Something happened – what if she couldn't get back in time? Did someone attack her? Here she was, running around on a silly Wild West adventure, not a care in the world. What was she thinking?

"How far do you think the drive is?"

Isabelle frowned. "To New York? More than 24 hours, I would say."

"That won't work," said Kayla. "I think I'll have to get the first flight out of Cody. Would you, and I'm sorry to spring this on you, but could you keep an eye on Oliver for me?"

"Of course! Anything you need, it's no problem."

Kayla thanked her and rushed onto her phone to buy a plane ticket. As she entered her credit card information, the thought dawned on her that this was a sure fire way to get in trouble with the Marshals. Also, she knew that Mitch would never forgive her.

It didn't matter, though. Her mom needed her. That was what mattered. If there was some mobster lurking around her apartment, waiting to ambush her, then so be it. She would face it when she got there.

Isabelle wished her luck and Kayla packed her things. It didn't take long, so then she sat on the couch, waiting anxiously. She was completely unable to sleep. In a weak moment, she used her Marshal issued cell phone to call both of her parents' phone numbers. No answer. At least now the Marshals would see what she was up to – if they didn't know already.

She got to the airport at 4 o'clock in the morning and got on a plane to Denver. From there, she took another plane to Albany and rented a car at the airport. Though she had hardly slept, she didn't feel tired; she was wired and focused.

Before driving from the airport to the hospital where she suspected that her mother was staying, she used a payphone to call both of her parents' cell phones again.

They didn't pick up, and both calls went straight to voicemail. Clearly they forgot to charge their phones, wherever they were.

There was only one hospital in the area, so Kayla hoped that she'd find her mom there. She prayed that her mom was okay. It was hard to prevent her mind from wandering to the worst case scenario, though.

When she got to the hospital, she was in a bit of a predicament. She knew how the privacy laws worked, and at any other hospital, it would've been difficult for her to find out if her mom were staying there. But Kayla often visited her patients at this hospital, and sometimes even personally drove them to the emergency room when they were being stubborn.

They knew her here. That had to be worth something. She got to the information desk and was met with a friendly face.

"Dr. Small! So good to see you – your hair looks great!"

Kayla smiled. "Hey Cindy, thanks. It's good to see you too. I just got news that my mom was in the hospital. Could you tell me where she is? Of course my dad never charges his cell phone and I haven't been able to get in contact with him."

Cindy's jaw dropped. "Of course! Let me look."

Kayla smiled. Even though it wasn't technically right by policy, she was glad that she could bend the rules sometimes.

After searching in the computer, Cindy wrote down a room number on a sticky note. "That's where she is, let me know if you need anything, okay?"

Kayla nodded. "Thanks Cindy."

She got into the elevator and pressed the button for the third floor. It was a general internal medicine floor, so it didn't give Kayla any clues as to what happened, but at least her mom wasn't in the ICU.

Or, a morbid voice in her head chimed, in the morgue.

Kayla gritted her teeth. She moved back home so she could be near her parents, but she wasn't there when they needed her most. She felt like a failure of a daughter.

The elevator doors opened to the third floor and Kayla stepped into the hallway. Her heart pounded in her chest as she tried to be pleasant and smile at everyone that she recognized on the floor. She made her way to room 303. Before walking in, she took a deep breath and knocked lightly on the open wooden door.

A voice called out, "Come in!"

Her heart leapt. It was her mom.

"Mom!" she said, her voice breaking.

There she was, sitting up in bed and picking at her lunch. "Honey! What are you doing here?"

Kayla threw her arms around her mom's neck. "What are *you* doing here? What happened?"

Her mom held her tightly in a hug, patting her on the back. "Oh, it was nothing. A little heart attack. Look at your hair, I love it!"

Kayla pulled away. Why was everyone so interested in her hair at a time like this?

"You had a heart attack? That's not nothing!"

She waved a hand. "I knew the signs of it right away thanks to my lovely daughter. You always told me that the signs would be different in a woman than in a man. And they were! I had a stomach ache, and then I threw up. I broke out in this cold sweat, and I had just a brief moment of chest pain. And then I realized what was going on. I knew that I had to get to the hospital."

Kayla couldn't help it – tears sprung from her eyes. She hadn't slept in more than 24 hours and her nerves were fried. Seeing her mom alive flooded her with emotions that she couldn't process.

"Oh honey, don't cry. It's okay," her mom said.

Kayla struggled through a sob. "No, it's not okay. I should have been here for you. What if..."

She held up a hand. "Don't start with the 'What if's.' Everything is fine. I'm fine! Your dad called 911, just like you taught us. They got me in here, they put two stents in my heart. I'm good as new!"

Something about imagining her mother in an ambulance made Kayla cry even harder. It was a full on ugly cry.

Her mother pulled her in for another hug. "It's okay honey. You're here now, and I'm going to be just fine."

Kayla sobbed for the next five minutes. For some reason, she couldn't stop. She understood what caused heart attacks. She knew about stents and how to treat a blockage. She could see that her mom was okay, but still somehow it was too overwhelming to deal with.

Her dad walked in the room to find her crying. "Look who it is! Our little criminal."

Kayla turned to him, surprised. "What?"

He laughed. "Did you really think that the FBI and the Marshals would keep us in the dark? They were afraid that you would come back to see your mom."

"Which you did," interjected her mother sternly. "Even though you shouldn't have."

Kayla blew her nose so she could talk more clearly. "Did they tell you everything?"

"No," her mom said. "Just that you saved some sort of a criminal and that you're in danger."

"I'm not sure how much danger I'm really in."

Her mother frowned. "They warned us that if you came here, they wouldn't be able to protect you."

"Oh mom," Kayla shook her head. "Please don't worry about it. I'll be fine. I was much more worried about you."

"And now I'm worried about you!"

Kayla's dad cut in. "All right you two loons, we can't all be worried all the time. Everyone is fine. Let's enjoy the extra peach cobbler that the nice lady gave me while Kayla tells us about her witness protection adventure."

Kayla felt like she was going to cry again for some reason. "I don't know where to begin."

Her mom took her hand. "Why don't you start from where you saved that man?"

She looked at her parents and smiled. That part was easy to tell. It was everything that came afterwards that became progressively more complicated.

At least she had lots of pictures of Oliver to share.

Chapter 19

That night, Mitch couldn't sleep. He wasn't going to give in and do what Kayla wanted him to do, but he wanted to find a way to explain to her why he felt so strongly about rejecting his dad's money.

Yes, he could donate it all to charity. He could use it to help people. It wasn't that he didn't understand that possibility – he felt like he had no right to the money in the first place. On top of that, there was something deeper. Darker. Something he didn't want to admit even to himself.

It was hard to explain to Kayla the shameful pit in his heart that made him wonder what he would be like if he had access to that much money. Would it turn him into his father? Would he, too, grow greedy and immoral?

Mitch never spoke those fears out loud to anyone. He never even fully admitted it to himself – not until Kayla forced him to think about what he was doing. Or rather, what he wasn't doing.

Though he didn't feel ready to talk to her about that, he decided to go to the ranch and apologize as soon as he could. It was only a week before his testimony, and he didn't want their friendship to end on bad terms. It hurt him enough to think that he could never speak to her again, but for her to leave angry with him on top of it? That was unbearable.

Early the next morning, he got dressed, drove over to the ranch, and knocked on her cabin door.

No answer.

He waited a minute before giving her a call. It went straight to voicemail. That was odd.

After popping his head into the stables, he checked the lodge to see if she stopped in to get breakfast. Isabelle stood at the front desk.

"Isabelle, have you seen Kayla around?"

"Oh," Isabelle replied, her cheery expression fading. "I guess you didn't hear. She left this morning."

He leaned on the counter. "Left? Where? Like on a trail ride? Or a trip to Yellowstone?"

Isabelle shook her head. "No, she had to go back home. She got news that her mom was sick. She got the first flight this morning."

Mitch felt a jolt of electricity run through his body. "That can't be. She's not safe on her own."

"What?" Isabelle gave him a puzzled look. "What do you mean?"

"I have to go," he said. "Please let me know if you hear anything else, okay?"

Isabelle could tell that he wasn't joking. "Okay, I will."

Was this some sort of trap set by Colin? How did Isabelle even hear that her mom was sick? Why didn't she just call her? Why didn't she call *him* before running off like that? He would've done anything to help her.

Mitch got back into his truck and dialed Perez's number.

She answered after two rings. "Hey Mitch, how's it going?"

"Not so good, I just heard that Kayla left Cody? Did you know about this?"

"Yeah, I did," Perez said with a sigh. "But not until after she was already gone. We knew that her mom was in the hospital, and we were afraid that she might try to go see her."

"What can we do? To protect her?"

There was a pause on the other end. "Unfortunately, there's nothing we can do."

Mitch couldn't believe what he was hearing. "She's a sitting duck out there! It's almost time for the testimony, I'm sure they're getting desperate."

"I'm sorry, but my hands are tied. We can't make any exceptions. Once somebody leaves our protection, we can't bring them back in, and we're not going to expose our agents to danger because she made a bad decision."

Mitch closed his eyes and tried to think.

"You still there?" asked Perez.

"Yeah, I'm here."

"Don't get any ideas. If you go after her, you'll both be in trouble. And we will not be able to help you. Do you understand?"

Mitch gritted his teeth. "Yeah, I know. I gotta go."

He hung up the phone. Mitch didn't care about putting himself in danger. His first instinct was to book a flight and chase after her, but the more he thought that plan through, the dumber it seemed.

First off, he was more recognizable than Kayla was. There could be tons of people looking for him, and if they found him, he might lead them straight to her. If he did manage to find her before anyone found him, she probably wouldn't agree to come back with him. She may still refuse to speak to him at all. And if they ran into trouble, Mitch wouldn't be able to protect her.

An idea hit him. There was someone that he trusted, someone that he knew could protect Kayla. He pulled out his phone and dialed the phone number that his dad made him memorize years ago.

A woman picked up. "Duchess Dry Cleaner, how can I help you?"

Mitch had to make sure that he got this right. He cleared his throat. "I'm looking for a three-piece pinstripe suit, and I need it this Sunday."

"You can expect it Sunday," the woman responded before disconnecting the call.

Mitch waited anxiously. Was it a three-piece pinstripe suit? Or was it a three-piece pinstripe tux? He knew it was something ridiculous. Luckily, a minute later, his phone rang.

"Hello?"

"Marty! Is that you?"

"No," Mitch said, lowering his voice. "It's his son."

There was silence for a moment. "Holy smokes kid, I haven't talked to you in ages."

"I know, Silver. I've been – well, living my own life."

"I heard about that," Silver replied, letting out a laugh. "Admire you for it, good for you for getting out."

Mitch shifted uncomfortably. "Thanks. But I need to ask you a favor. I've got someone who needs 24 hour protection, starting immediately. She's in Albany. Can you help?"

Silver let out a long sigh. "For how long?"

"At least a week. Maybe more."

"Hm." He was silent for a moment.

Mitch wanted to yell at him, but he knew he had to play it cool. Silver was retired CIA, and he was a good guy. If Silver was willing to take the job, he would do it well, no questions asked. If he wasn't willing to, though, there was nothing that would convince him to accept it. He was not a guy who could be convinced of anything.

"All right, I'll get a team together. Fifty thousand for the week."

There was just over fifty five thousand dollars in Mitch's savings – the downpayment for his future home. "Perfect. Let me get you the details."

"You got it kid."

Chapter 20

The excitement of telling her parents about Wyoming gave Kayla some energy to overcome her exhaustion from not sleeping. She told them all about the fundraiser, the ranch, Isabelle, how she learned to put a bridle on a horse, the first time she got stepped on by a horse, and square dancing.

They loved the pictures of Oliver and couldn't wait to meet their new grand puppy. Kayla gave them a full overview of Buffalo Bill and the history of the area – her mom was delighted to hear that Wyoming was the first state in the union to allow women to vote.

The one thing that she didn't give a lot of detail about was Mitch. And of course, her mom noticed.

"What about that guy? The one that you were there with?"

Kayla tried to keep her tone even. "What about him?"

"Well, what was he like?" Her mother casually straightened the blanket over her legs. "You spent a lot of time with him. Was he a nice guy?"

"Not *that* much time," she said with a shrug. "But yeah, I guess he was nice."

"Did you see him pretty often?"

"Well, I was supposed to see him at least two or three times a week, but I needed to use the internet on his computer for the fundraiser, so I saw him almost every day for a while. It turned out that I did have internet, I just didn't know it until the night that I left."

Her mom eyed her for a moment. "Oh, right. When will you see him again?"

Kayla paused. Why were moms so observant? How did she pick up on Kayla's unwillingness to talk about Mitch?

And though she didn't check, she knew that she was probably kicked out of the witness protection program. If she went back to the ranch now and told the truth about her stay, it could put Mitch in danger. She needed to go back to get Oliver of course, but she realized that she may never see Mitch again.

"I...don't know," she finally said. The realization sunk in her heart like a deflated balloon. "I think he has to, you know, stay in hiding."

"Oh," her father said. "He gets to be a cowboy forever."

"Yeah," Kayla said weakly. For some reason, she felt tired again. "Mom, it's getting late, and you need to get some rest. I think I'll head home and get some rest too, but I'll be back in the morning, okay?"

Her mother held up a finger in protest. "Now wait one minute. We can't let you go home all by yourself if there are men looking for you."

Kayla sighed. "Mom. No one tried to grab me the whole way here. I doubt that anyone is even looking for me anymore."

"Nevertheless, I think you should go home with dad."

Kayla groaned. "I really just wanted to sleep in my own bed tonight. And what's dad going to do if someone attacks me? Jeopardy trivia them to death?"

Her dad made a face of mock outrage. "How do you know that wouldn't work?"

"Please honey," her mom said. "I'd feel much better if you were with your father."

It wasn't worth her mom staying up all night worrying. "Alright, if it'll help you get some rest."

They said their goodbyes and Kayla drove home, following closely behind her dad. She kept an eye out on the road for any suspicious vehicles following them. There was nothing. She laughed at herself – she was starting to feel like Mitch. He was always paranoid and worried something would happen. And all the worrying was all for naught.

When they got home, Kayla took a hot shower and went straight to bed; she fell asleep almost immediately even though her childhood twin bed was fairly lumpy.

The next morning, she woke up from a bad dream about Mitch. She wanted to avoid thinking about it, so she got up and made coffee for herself and her dad. She offered to make him breakfast as well, but he wanted to get to the hospital early because it was the day her mom was supposed to be discharged home.

"Okay dad, let me just throw on some clothes and I'll go with you," she said.

He gave her a kiss on the forehead. "No sweetie, I'm just going to run over, pick up your mom, and come right back home. You still look tired. Just wait here, it won't take very long."

Kayla frowned. She didn't like being left out. Plus, she had a hard time controlling her thoughts that morning after waking up from that upsetting dream.

Why was she dreaming about Mitch? In the dream, his junky rental house was literally falling apart around him, yet he refused to spend any money to fix it. Kayla pleaded with him, telling him he had to at least fix the roof that leaked directly into his bedroom.

"No," he kept repeating, "you just don't understand."

She woke up irritated with him. But then she couldn't stop thinking about him, which was even more annoying.

Luckily, there was a lot that she could do at the house to distract herself and to prepare for her mom's arrival. "I guess I could wash all of these dishes that you left here for mom. She won't like coming home to a dirty kitchen."

He laughed. "You two notice everything. I wasn't going to waste time washing a few pots and pans while she was in the hospital!"

Kayla patted him on the shoulder. "Sure dad, I know that you would've jumped at the chance to wash dishes at any other time."

He winked at her and left through the garage.

Kayla busied herself with tidying up the kitchen. She washed all of the dishes and set them to dry. Next, she sorted the mail into more manageable piles for her mom to address when she got home. After taking out the trash, she wiped off the counters and the kitchen table before grabbing the vacuum cleaner.

There likely wasn't much time before her parents got back, but she wanted to make it as nice as possible. Vacuuming always took the longest because her parents still had the same ancient, heavy vacuum from when she lived there in high school. She couldn't believe it still worked. It was so loud that she could barely hear herself humming.

At one point, she thought that she heard a door open. She turned off the vacuum immediately, and stood there listening in the silence, her heart pounding. Did someone get into the house? She was really getting paranoid now.

She quietly reached for her cell phone and waited. After two minutes, she didn't hear anything. She shook her head and sighed. It wasn't worth living the rest of her life worrying about sounds that she imagined while vacuuming. She'd have to relax eventually.

She restarted the vacuum and wheeled it into the living room. It took about ten minutes to do a good job in there, and by the end she noticed that the vacuum looked pretty full. She decided it was best to empty it before she took it upstairs. She bent over, detached the dustbin, and spun around to go back to the kitchen.

Suddenly, there was a hand over her mouth.

"Don't scream, and don't make this worse," said the man restraining her.

She dropped the dustbin and instinctively screamed. It was muffled and useless under his grip. Another person grabbed her hands, securing her wrists with a zip tie.

"We've been looking everywhere for you Dr. Small."

He said her name with such disdain that it sent chills down her spine.

Her heart thundered in her chest. How was this possible? How could these idiots think that she was involved with Marty and be desperate enough to kidnap her?

Unable to speak, she settled with narrowing her eyes at him.

He laughed. "Oh, what's the matter? Did you need to finish cleaning up around here?"

Kayla tried to respond but there was now tape over her mouth.

"Don't be scared sweetheart," he said, staring at her with joy glowing from his beady eyes.

Kayla was at least six inches taller than him, and she peered down at his shining, bald head. The guy looked like such a dweeb – like someone who would try to cut in front of her at the grocery store and act surprised if he were called out on it. His sidekick looked no older than eighteen. Yet somehow they still managed to sneak up on her.

She wasn't scared. She was angry.

"Come on Dr. *Tall*," he said, with what sounded like a snort, as he led her to the back door. "We've got a lot of catching up to do."

They stepped through the door and into the backyard. Almost immediately, a voice called out, "Police! Hands up, get on the ground!"

Her two kidnappers immediately fell to their knees. Kayla looked down at them, bewildered. It was happening too fast for her to process.

Police officers descended upon the kidnappers and a man with gray hair approached her.

"Hi Kayla, are you alright?"

She didn't know how to respond. The police seemed preoccupied with the criminals – which was fine by her. This guy wasn't dressed like an officer, but the only way he'd know that name would be if he knew her from witness protection. Was he FBI?

She decided he must be safe and nodded.

He swiftly cut her hands free so she could remove the tape from her mouth. "Thank you."

"My name is Silver, it's nice to meet you."

Kayla smiled. She felt like she was in a daze. "Hi Silver."

"I'm sorry that this happened to you. The good news is that we might have gotten enough intelligence to really get these guys in trouble."

"That's nice." She wanted to listen to what this man had to say, but it dawned on her that her parents could arrive at any minute. If her mom saw their home surrounded by police, she would have another heart attack. "Is it okay if I give my parents a call to let them know that everything is okay?"

He nodded. "Of course."

She took a deep breath and stepped a few feet away from the excitement. The flashing lights atop the police cars blinded her and made the situation seem even more surreal.

What was she even going to say to her parents? She called her dad, and luckily, he picked up. He told her that her mom's discharge was delayed because the cardiologist wanted to see her one last time, but he was called into an emergency case that morning. They wouldn't be home for another few hours.

Kayla was relieved. It'd be best to tell them everything in person; she decided that for the time being, she'd tell them that the police came by, but everything was okay and she'd explain later.

Unlike her mom, her dad wasn't one to ask too many questions. "Sounds good sweetie, you stay safe and we'll be home soon."

She felt a bit calmer after hanging up – at least her mom wouldn't be scared half to death when she got home. Kayla turned around to look for Silver, but he was nowhere to be seen. Instead, one of the police officers approached her.

"Hi Dr. Small, my name is Sergeant Blair. We got a tip that you were in danger, and I'm glad we got here when we did. Are you okay?"

"Yes," she said, her voice oddly calm. "I'm totally fine. Thank you for coming and..." Her voice broke. Maybe she wasn't as calm as she thought.

"You're very welcome. We're going to get these two down to the station, but maybe you and I can go inside, and I can clarify a bit of what's going on?"

"Sure, come on in," Kayla said as though she were inviting him in for lemonade. She must've still been in shock, because none of it felt real.

And for some reason, Mitch's face kept popping up into her head. And not in an "I told you so" kind of way. It wasn't even that she was worried that he was in danger – that wasn't quite it. It was like she couldn't stop thinking about the fact that she'd never see him again, as though that would be the worst part of being kidnapped.

Odd how brains work, she thought airily as she opened the back door for Sergeant Blair.

"Can I make you some tea?" she asked him.

"Uh sure, that'd be nice," he said, nodding to a few officers to follow him and stand guard.

Chapter 21

Waiting for news from Silver was torture. Though Mitch trusted Silver, somehow he couldn't shake the awful feeling that something might happen to Kayla.

He drove back to his house and got on the computer. He was supposed to work a shift selling insurance, but he couldn't think straight. Instead of taking calls, he bought a plane ticket to Albany. He couldn't leave Kayla to fend for herself.

Not half an hour later, his phone rang. It was Perez.

"Hello?"

"Mitch, how's it going?"

There was a chance, of course, that the Marshals didn't know what he was thinking. But he knew that chance was slim. "I'm getting ready to find Kayla."

She laughed. "Oh, I did not expect you to say that."

Surely the Marshals could see his every move? "Oh, I thought you knew."

"I did, but I'm surprised by your honesty."

Mitch sighed. "I understand that you won't be able to provide me protection once I leave. But this is my decision."

"Actually, it isn't. We're only a week away from your testimony, and a lot of our case rests on it. We can't let you leave Cody."

"What do you mean you can't let me? I'm a free man."

"Yes," she said patiently, "you are free. But I'm telling you right now, if you leave and are hurt or prevented from testifying, your dad will still go to jail, but it's likely that many of the other people involved in his crimes will walk free."

Mitch buried his face in his hands. He still couldn't believe that his testimony was so important, but from what the FBI told him earlier, his knowledge established years of criminal connections. He understood that it was important, but nothing was more important than Kayla. His own life was worth nothing if Kayla was harmed.

"Are you still there?" asked Perez.

"Yeah," he replied. "I am. I'm just thinking."

"Listen, there isn't much that we can do right now for Kayla. But I will reach out to the local police department and make sure that they're on the lookout for Colin and his gang. I'll let them know how serious it is."

"That's something," he said.

"This will sound harsh," she said slowly, "but I'm pretty sure that if you show your face in Albany, it will only draw more attention to her. They'll think that she's around, too."

That thought crossed his mind initially, but after sitting and replaying his worst fears, he pushed it to the side and decided to go anyway. "I can see that."

"And don't think you can trade yourself to save her. They'll take you both. Stay put. I'll do everything I can. Please don't do anything stupid, and I will keep you updated, okay?"

Mitch rubbed his eyes. The last thing he wanted to do was make it worse for her, especially if she wasn't even on Colin's radar anymore. He could get there and make everything worse. "All right, thank you."

Unable to focus, Mitch went out to his workshop to do something with his hands. Anything to distract him for the rest of the day.

It didn't work that well, but it was better than nothing. Around eight that evening, he got a call from Silver. He had a bit of news – his team was in place and succeeded in locating Kayla. They watched her as she left the airport, got to the hospital, and left the hospital. The team was conducting 24 hour surveillance and would not let her out of their sight. Silver said that they detected some suspicious activity.

"What kind of activity?" asked Mitch impatiently. "Have they told the police yet?"

Silver took a long breath. "Not yet. She's not in any danger. She has a guy watching her, and as soon as he makes his move, the team will make sure the police are right there."

"*After* he makes a move? Why can't they catch him before that? She could get hurt."

"She won't," Silver said flatly. "We've seen much tougher cases than one woman being followed by one guy. If we grab him before he does anything, the police won't be able to hold him. You know this, stop thinking so much with your heart."

Mitch's face flushed red. That was not normally something that he would be accused of. He tended to be a logical person. "If anything happens to her –"

Silver cut him off. "It won't. Stop worrying. I'll update you in the morning."

The line disconnected. Mitch had the urge to drop his phone in the trash and book another flight to Albany. If it was just one guy, Mitch could definitely take him. He wasn't a trained fighter or anything, but he could throw a few punches or something. Anything.

Mitch had another sleepless night. He kept thinking about Kayla – and not just about her being in danger, but about all the adventures they'd had together over the past few weeks. As guilty as he felt that she was dragged into the witness protection program with him, he was also extremely grateful.

If it weren't for her, he would never have taken the initiative to get to know so many people in town. He never would've gone square dancing and he probably would've never gone to Yellowstone. Had she never come, he might be better at selling insurance, but everything else in his life would've been worse.

Kayla could bring sunshine into any situation; she was unwaveringly positive and incredibly fun. It was no wonder that she made friends everywhere she went. She was smart and funny, generous and kind...she was unlike anyone he'd ever met.

Mitch felt like he was being driven mad with guilt. Guilt that something might happen to her and it would be his fault. Guilt that he didn't listen to her and give more consideration into taking his dad's money; so the last time they saw each other, she wasn't speaking to him.

Why didn't he just tell her that he was afraid of becoming consumed by greed, like his father? Kayla wasn't a judgmental person. She wouldn't have thought less of him. She probably could've talked him through it.

Instead, he kept it all to himself. Now he would never see her again, and she might even end up hurt because of him. After a few hours of worrying, he fell into a restless sleep plagued with nightmares of dark shadows following Kayla through the hallways of the hospital.

He was awoken the next morning by the ring of his cell phone. It was Silver. Mitch felt his heart rate go through the roof.

"Hey, what's going on?"

"Everything is good," said Silver. "Everything is really good."

"Is Kayla okay? What happened?"

"She's completely fine. The guy – Colin – made a move to take her, but we knew it was coming, and had the police waiting for him."

Mitch swallowed. Take her? "He actually *got* her?"

"He did, but the entire ordeal was less than ten minutes from the time he entered the house until he left the house and got arrested. Just enough time to catch him red-handed."

"Was she hurt?"

"No, not at all. We bugged the house so we knew exactly what was going on. I gave the tapes to the police to build their case."

Mitch felt the tightness in his chest easing up just a bit. "That's good."

Silver continued. "It is. Turns out that Colin demanded a pretty high price to track down your girl. It was so high that five of your dad's old partners pitched in to pay him. And Colin is singing to the police like a canary."

Mitch let out a sigh. "You're kidding."

Silver laughed. "No, totally serious. He's giving them everything. Names, billing statements, wire transfers. The cops will arrest them in the next 24 hours, and then your girl will never have anything to worry about again."

He kept calling her "his girl." That wasn't quite true, but Mitch didn't correct him. "That's incredible."

"I told you that we know what we're doing," said Silver smugly. "I like to set a trap before I intervene. This Colin wasn't a very bright guy."

Mitch cracked a smile. "Doesn't seem like it, does it?"

"Do you still want the team watching her for the rest of the week?"

"Absolutely. But don't scare her."

"You got it. Alright, I gotta run. Take it easy."

"Thanks. See you."

Mitch set his phone on the bedside table. He felt like he was floating. Kayla was safe, and she was going to be okay. It turned out that Silver was the right guy to call after all. And with the police, and hopefully soon the FBI and Marshals, on her side again, she was in good hands.

A weight lifted from his chest. *Kayla was okay.* The only thing that would make it better would be if he could see her again and explain how sorry he was. He knew it was impossible, though.

A smart, beautiful and sassy woman walked into his life, and he messed it up. He was his usual quiet self and kept all of his thoughts and feelings locked up. He allowed fear to dictate how he behaved – fear of being judged, fear of her leaving forever. It didn't matter in the end, he still ended up with a broken heart.

Mitch bitterly wished that he would have at least told her how he felt about her. If only he hadn't been so afraid.

Chapter 22

The police cleared out after a few hours, and Kayla's mom arrived home later that evening. It was perfect timing; Kayla could calmly explain that she was sort of, kind of abducted, but the police were fully aware of what was going on and were able to rescue her.

Unfortunately, her mother didn't find that very comforting. "I can't believe this happened! I am never having a heart attack again!"

"Great, I was hoping you'd say that," said Kayla.

Her mother let out a huff. "How can you be so calm? Something bad could've happened. Something bad did happen!"

Kayla sighed. She'd always taken after her father – it took a lot to ruffle his feathers, and he sat in the corner of the room with a slightly amused look on his face.

"Nothing bad happened," Kayla said. "In fact, it was actually pretty lucky that he abducted me. The sergeant told me that they now have enough evidence to track down all of the guys that were looking for me, and because a crime was actually committed, they'll go to jail."

Her dad chimed in. "See? She's even safer than she would've been if she wasn't kidnapped. Sometimes kidnapping is a good thing."

Her mother shot him a dirty look. She remained unconvinced, but she was grateful that everyone was okay.

It took a bit, but Kayla convinced her mom that it was safe enough for her to travel back to Cody and pick up Oliver. She missed him terribly, and since the Marshals deactivated her phone, she wasn't able to get in contact with Isabelle.

Somehow, not only did they cut off service to the phone, they rendered it completely useless. It wouldn't turn on and she couldn't access any of her contacts. A few times she considered calling the ranch directly to check on Oliver, but she still didn't want to blow Mitch's cover. He was still in danger. Probably. She didn't know, because that guy from the FBI hadn't come around to talk to her again. What was his name? Bronze? No – Silver.

Her flight to Wyoming went much more quickly compared to when she flew to Albany to see her mom. She was even able to sleep a little bit. Her plan was to rent a car for the trip back and drive to Albany; initially she wanted to fly, but she didn't think that Oliver would do very well on a plane. His anxiety would be uncontrollable. He kind of reminded her of her mom in a funny way. Maybe that's why they got along so well.

When she got to the ranch, she half expected the Marshals to swoop in and tell her that she had to leave. Luckily, nothing like that happened. The ranch was unchanged. Guests milled about, the sun shined, and a handsome wrangler addressed a new group of horseback riders. Kayla didn't recognize him, and she had enough trouble with handsome wranglers, so she decided to avoid any introductions.

She walked past him and on to her cabin; she couldn't wait to see Oliver. When she opened the front door, though, Oliver wasn't there. His crate remained, along with his bowl and his toys, but there was no sign of him.

After checking the stables, she went to the lodge to look for Isabelle, but she wasn't around. Kayla asked the person manning the front desk where Isabelle was, but they didn't know.

Maybe Isabelle had taken Oliver for a walk. Kayla decided to go back to her cabin and wait on the porch.

Two hours later, there was still no word of Isabelle or Oliver. She didn't want to overreact, but she was starting to get worried.

Finally, after waiting for three hours, she caught sight of Isabelle.

"Hey!" she yelled from the porch.

Isabelle excused herself from the group of guests that she was talking to. She ran over and threw her arms around Kayla's neck. "I'm so glad to see you! Is everything okay?"

"Yes," Kayla said, hugging her fiercely. "My mom is okay. She had a heart attack, but she's home now and doing well. I'm sorry I haven't been in touch – my phone is broken and things have been a little crazy."

Isabelle beamed. "That's okay, I'm just glad that your mom is okay and that you're okay."

"Thanks. I went to my cabin to look for Oliver, but he wasn't there. Did you have to move him? Was he being destructive?"

"What do you mean? I thought that..." Isabelle's voice trailed off.

Uh oh. "You thought what?"

Isabelle covered her mouth with her hand as the color drained from her face. "I can't believe I'm so stupid. George said that – you know."

Kayla felt her heart rate beginning to quicken. "George said what? Does he have Oliver?"

"I think so? He stopped by yesterday and said that you'd asked him to take Oliver to meet you."

"To meet me where? I haven't talked to George since I left. Where is he?"

"I don't know." Isabelle's round brown eyes started to fill with tears. "He left in a hurry, he said there were some problems at home and that he was going to meet you on the way. I tried to call you, but your phone wasn't working."

Of course. George must've left town, realizing that his scheming days in Cody were over. And no doubt he must've figured out who was responsible for his demise. Kayla felt her knees grow weak; would he really be so awful to steal her dog to get back at her?

"Kayla? Are you okay? You don't look so good."

"I think I just need to sit down." She turned back to the front steps of her cabin.

Isabelle followed. "I'm so sorry! Why would George lie about that?"

As much as Kayla wanted to explain it to her, when she opened her mouth, all that came out was a sob. She started crying hysterically. Her mom survived a heart attack, and she survived being kidnapped. Could Oliver survive being dog-napped by George?

Maybe he dropped him off at an animal shelter. Or maybe he dropped him off in the middle of nowhere. How would Kayla ever find him?

After crying for a good ten minutes, Kayla calmed down enough to tell Isabelle about George's criminal record.

Isabelle kept apologizing, but Kayla interrupted her. "No. It's my fault. I thought it was safer not to tell you, so the police could handle it before he did any more damage. But of course I should've told you. He was working here, you deserved to know. It's my own fault that he was able to get away with Ollie."

A few tears slipped down Isabelle's face. She wiped them away impatiently. "Well, he can't have gone far. We'll get a search party together and go looking for him. Let me call Mitch, I'm sure he'll want to help too."

"No!" Kayla said quickly. "I don't – I can't see him right now. I'd prefer we just gather some people to look for Oliver."

Isabelle gave her a funny look but didn't ask any questions.

They were able to pull together a group of almost thirty people; some, including Kayla, were on horseback. They combed the area around the ranch until dark, but they had no luck in finding him.

Kayla checked with the local animal shelters, but no dogs matched Oliver's description. She spent the next five days looking for him to no avail. She was heartbroken, devastated and full of bitter guilt.

On her sixth day in Cody, Kayla woke up early to get ready for another long day of searching. She was just about to leave her cabin when she heard a knock at the front door. She peeked through the window – it was that Silver guy.

"Good morning," she said as she opened the door.

He tipped his hat. For some reason he was now wearing a cowboy hat. "Morning Kayla. Do you mind if I come in?"

Her first thought was that yes, she did mind and she didn't want to deal with any more strangers that might kidnap her. Then she realized that if he wanted to kidnap her, he probably wouldn't have knocked on her front door. "Sure, why not."

He walked in and took a seat on her couch. Kayla sat across from him.

"How can I help you?" she asked. "Did the FBI find my dog?"

He pursed his lips. "I wouldn't be privy to that information."

She drew back slightly. If this guy wasn't FBI, who was he?

As though reading her mind, he said, "I'm not with the FBI. But I am on your side."

"Is that right?" Kayla felt the muscles in her body tighten. "Because I have no idea who you are."

He smiled. Did he find her amusing? She certainly wasn't amused by him.

"I come in peace, I swear," he said, holding his hands up. "I was hired by your friend – Mitch? Is that what he's going by now?"

"What? Why would Mitch hire you?"

"To keep you alive," Silver said flatly.

She crossed her arms but didn't know how to respond.

Silver continued. "Didn't you wonder how the police knew the exact moment that Colin kidnapped you?"

Kayla shrugged. Truth be told, she assumed the Marshals were watching Colin and saw what he was doing or something.

"I figured that he got caught because he was an idiot," she offered.

Silver chuckled. "He was an idiot, but that didn't stop him from almost succeeding in his goal. No Kayla, my team and I have been watching you from the moment you stepped off the plane in Albany."

"What! There's no way. I would've noticed."

"I spent thirty years of my life working for the CIA. I got bored of my retirement and decided to put together a team with specialized skills, one of them being surveillance and protection. Do you really think you would've noticed being watched by us if you didn't even notice Colin following you?"

Kayla frowned. He had a point. "I guess not."

Silver clapped his hands together. "Exactly. No offense to you, it's just not a skill that you've ever had to work on before."

That did make her feel a bit better. "Yeah, that's true."

"I've known Mitch for a long time. Almost his whole life. His dad and I go way back. So when he called me and asked me to protect you, I didn't hesitate."

Kayla's eyes grew wide. "Why did he want to protect me? I thought he would hate me for leaving Wyoming."

Silver stared at her for a moment before responding. "I don't believe that's the case. He spared no expense to make sure that you were safe. And clearly, you needed it."

Kayla pinched her lips. She didn't exactly like this Silver character. At the same time, though, the fact that Mitch wanted to protect her made her feel hopeful. Could that mean that he didn't actually hate her for what she did?

If Mitch hadn't gotten help for her, she may have actually been kidnapped. Her heart sank. She should've listened to him about how serious this all was. She should've listened to him about a lot of things.

Silver went on. "And now, he is one day away from testifying in court against his father. And you're not there to support him?"

"I – " She stopped. The timing made sense, but she never knew any details about the trial. She didn't even know Mitch's real name. "I had no idea."

Silver stared at her.

She felt pressured to speak again. "And I need to find my dog. This guy George stole him, and I don't know what he may have done to him."

"That is unfortunate," Silver said with a nod. "And we've also been looking for your dog. We had no choice, since we're still following you around. Which you also didn't notice."

She really *was* bad at knowing that she was being followed.

"Well – thank you for your help."

"You're welcome. That dog isn't around here, though. You're going to have to find George Walters himself to get your dog back."

Kayla's heart sank. She was afraid that might be the case. "Oh."

"And if you get on a plane in the next eight hours, you'll make it to Mitch's testimony. But if you don't..."

She let the silence hang in the air. Kayla took her eyes off of Silver; his stare made her uncomfortable. It felt like he was looking into her soul. It was not a pleasant feeling.

"I can't just leave Cody and abandon Oliver to the grizzlies."

Silver stood up, straightening his shirt. "Who said anything about abandoning? Like I said, it's highly unlikely that your dog is here. You're wasting your time. And quite frankly, ours."

Kayla stood to follow him. "Is it even safe for me to appear at the trial? Isn't that kind of like a turkey walking into Thanksgiving dinner?"

"Nope. We took care of all of your enemies. I mean – they're going to jail, not that we – uh, you know, did anything to them. They'd be fools to approach you now. Anyway, it's too late."

Kayla winced. She didn't like this crime stuff. "Right."

Silver put his hand on the door. "Think about it. I'll be seeing you."

And with that, he walked out of the door and into the bright morning.

Kayla stood there stunned. What was she supposed to do with all of this information?

Chapter 23

They were stuck in a stare off.

Agent Simmons let out a sigh. He looked at Marshal Perez; she said nothing. Neither did Mitch.

He sat across from them, arms folded over his chest. Mitch was never the kind of person to insist on getting his way. For most things, he was very easy going. He never needed to be the one to pick the restaurant or the movie when he spent time with friends. Never in his life did he ask to speak to a manager or file a complaint.

This was different. It was something too important to let slide.

Mitch stretched his shoulders as though he were settling in for a long wait. Finally, Perez spoke.

"Even if we could find George, there's no guarantee that we'll have him apprehended before the trial today."

Mitch leaned forward. "If he's located, and there is a plan to arrest him, I will testify."

Simmons abruptly stood up.

"Where are you going?" asked Perez.

"I'm going to get a good team together. The clock is ticking, and I need to catch a cowboy."

Perez watched as he left the room. She took a sip of her coffee before throwing the disposable cup into the trash. "I guess I better get to work too, then."

Mitch nodded. "Thank you."

Even though he was refusing to testify unless Oliver was found, there was no need to be impolite about it. He watched as Perez left the room.

The night before, Silver sent Mitch a disguised email to let him know that Kayla was safe and that she was staying in Cody. He spoke in code, so it was a bit confusing, but Mitch was able to figure out that Oliver was missing and the culprit appeared to be George.

His first instinct was to fly back to Cody and find Oliver on his own. Yet he knew that Kayla, and subsequently Silver and his team, looked for Oliver for days with no luck. Clearly, George left the area. The FBI lost track of him, too, before they were able to arrest him for his history of scams.

If there was one thing that Mitch knew well, it was crooks. He knew that George wouldn't be able to lay low for any significant period of time. He'd think he was smarter than everyone looking for him and that he could set up his scheme in another town without being detected.

Mitch knew that there was a ranch or farm somewhere that just gained a new employee, and he insisted that the FBI find out where. Immediately after getting Silver's message, he told the agents his new demands.

At first they said no, which Mitch expected. He was fully prepared to follow through on his threat and planned to take matters into his own hands. He was confident that he'd be able to find George eventually.

He just knew that the FBI would be able to do it a lot faster. And honestly, better. Mitch was impressed with how they worked; he found himself fantasizing about a career of catching crooks instead of selling insurance.

He spent the next five hours pacing in his room. They didn't provide any updates about their search and Mitch was half tempted to start his search for George early.

With only thirty minutes before he had to leave for the trial, Simmons walked in the door with an update.

"We found him," he said breathlessly. "We tracked him to a farm in Montana."

A smile broke across Mitch's face. "I knew you could do it."

He pulled out a surveillance photo. It was clearly George, though his hair was dyed black.

"This was him one day ago at a gas station one mile from the farm. We confirmed with the owner that they hired him and he started this week."

"He works fast, doesn't he?"

"Not as fast as us," Simmons replied with a smile.

"Does he still have Oliver?" asked Mitch.

"We're not sure yet," Simmons said slowly. "But we have a team of agents flying to Montana right now. They'll initiate the arrest, and if Oliver is there, we'll bring him back."

Mitch frowned. That wasn't ideal.

Simmons sensed his hesitation. "It's the best we can do right now. The agents will land in five hours. *Please* tell me that you'll go testify."

"Oh," said Mitch with surprise. "Yes, I will. Of course. I'm just thinking...if Oliver is there, he'll be terrified of the agents. Maybe Kayla can go with them?"

Simmons shook his head. "Sorry, she can't. Since she was removed from witness protection, we can't take her with us."

"Then can I go? He trusts me a little bit."

"Sure. Whatever it takes to get you to testify today. As soon as you're done, we'll get you on a plane."

Mitch extended his hand. "Deal."

The Marshals transported Mitch to the courthouse in a bullet-proof van, then snuck him through some underground hallways to get him into the courtroom unseen. They told him they were confident that his most dangerous foes would soon be in jail for their role in kidnapping Kayla, but they didn't want to take any chances. He stayed with two agents in a small room until it was time for him to make his big debut.

When Mitch walked into the courtroom, he couldn't help noticing how drab it looked compared to the courtrooms on TV. It was so ordinary – just a large room filled with people. It didn't have the grand wooden banisters and tall judge stand that he'd seen on *Law and Order*. Yet still, the judge seemed quite intimidating.

He tried not to think too much about that as he walked to the front. He made eye contact with his dad – he looked well and smiled at him as he passed.

Mitch felt a pang of guilt, but reminded himself that his father didn't blame him for what he was doing. The stubborn man refused to take a plea deal, though, just as he refused to turn in any of his business associates.

Mitch reached the front of the courtroom and turned around. For a moment, he thought his eyes were playing tricks on him. There was a woman towards the back who looked just like Kayla. But it couldn't be.

He squinted, trying to get a better look at her. She smiled and did a little wave.

It *was* her. He felt his breath catch in his lungs – he never thought that he would see her again. He smiled back.

For the first time, he was glad that he made it to this trial.

Chapter 24

Did he see? Kayla thought that Mitch looked right at her.

She felt her cheeks flush. Why did she decide to wave? What an awkward thing to do. Did that make him smile, though? It made it feel like her stomach was full of jello.

He must've seen her.

Mitch took the stand.

"Please stand. Raise your right hand. Do you promise that the testimony you shall give in the case before this court shall be the truth, the whole truth, and nothing but the truth, so help you God?"

Mitch's voice boomed across the room. "I do."

"Please state your first and last name."

"Jason Brash."

"You may take a seat."

Interesting. This entire time, Mitch never once told her his real name. He didn't look like a Jason. He was definitely a Mitch, and would remain a Mitch in her mind.

Kayla did her best to keep up with the questioning pouring from the prosecution. They employed a series of large poster boards, showing how webs of people were connected. They carefully went through each connection and Mitch described how he knew the person, when his father did business with them, and what sort of scheme they worked on together.

Kayla couldn't keep any of it straight, and she was amazed that Mitch could. He testified about keeping electronic records of all of his dad's contacts and plans. Kayla finally understood why he was so important to this trial – he connected all the dots.

Mitch's testimony went on for over an hour. The defense tried to discredit him, but Mitch kept his cool.

"How do we know that all of this isn't some sort of a tale that you cooked up to get back at your dad? I'm sure he wasn't the best dad, but is making all of this up fair revenge?"

Mitch didn't break eye contact. "You have all of the documents that I kept for my father. I'm not trying to get back at him. But what he did was wrong."

"So you admit that you want to get revenge?"

"No. Not at all."

"You want the jury to believe that you just had a change of heart after helping your father for all those years?"

Mitch looked down, then at his father before he spoke again. "I stopped helping my father years ago once I realized what he was doing. I still love him. It's not easy for me to speak out, but he hurt a lot of people."

It isn't easy for him to speak out in any situation, thought Kayla. A chill ran down her spine. If only the jury knew how true that was – but how could they? He was quiet and had that ever brooding face. He could easily come across as mean and judgmental to someone who didn't know him.

But he wasn't mean or judgmental at all. He was just...reserved. A private, but not bitter, person. She wished she could testify to his character, tell them about the chair leg that he made for her and how great he was with her timid dog.

Everything about him was so unlike what she'd known from guys before. He was kind and gentle; he was thoughtful and smart. He worried too much – that was for sure – but he had a good heart.

Was it all fake, though? Was it possible that, like Vera suggested, he liked her at one point and was only nice to her for that reason?

No – that didn't make sense. Mitch was nice to everyone else, too. Like John – he treated John and Vera like old friends and never hesitated to lend them a helping hand.

She didn't know if he ever liked her, but she knew that now he surely didn't. He probably despised her for ditching witness protection.

Except...he sent Silver to protect her after she left. Clearly, Mitch must've cared about her to do that.

Or, she thought ruefully, he knew she was a screw up who would blow his cover if left unchecked.

The defense rested their case after several more failed statements. They didn't have much to throw at Mitch, and Mitch was completely unflappable. Once he was dismissed, a few men in black suits rose to escort him out of the back door.

Kayla wanted to follow him out of the room. She wasn't sure if the Marshals would interpret that as some sort of threat, but it was a risk she was willing to take.

She quietly slid out of her seat and followed them out of the courtroom. Once the door was shut behind them, she called out.

"Mitch!"

She kept her distance in case yelling his name prompted one of the Marshals to tase her. That was definitely something she wanted to avoid.

Mitch turned around and once he spotted her, smiled broadly. "Kayla, how are you?"

He walked towards her, the Marshals following closely behind, betraying no emotion on their faces.

"I'm good. I mean – you know."

"How's your mom? Is she okay?"

The genuine concern in his eyes made Kayla feel something burn in her chest. Of course Mitch wasn't angry at her. How could she even have thought that he would be angry? She had him wrong all of this time. So wrong. And now it was too late.

"She's doing well, thank you. She had a heart attack, but she's getting better now."

Mitch nodded. "I'm so sorry to hear that. I'm glad that she's okay."

"Thank you. Me too."

One of the Marshals cleared his throat. "We need to get moving sir."

Mitch looked over his shoulder and motioned for them to wait a moment.

"I heard about the attempted abduction. I'm so sorry that happened –"

Kayla covered her eyes with her hand. "That was totally my fault. You were right all along. I should've been more careful, but at least nothing happened. In fact, it seems like a few more people will be going to jail. So I'll never have to worry about it again."

He smiled. "A blessing in disguise."

"Yeah, I think so." She searched his green eyes, looking for more confirmation that he wasn't angry with her. Or that he was...happy to see her? Or something. Anything. This might be the last time she'd ever see him.

The Marshal cleared his throat again.

"Well," Mitch said, "it was lovely to see you. But I think I'm being kicked out."

She forced a smile. "Right, I understand. Take care, okay?"

"You too."

He turned around and walked down the hallway.

Kayla couldn't get over the nauseous feeling in her stomach. Why was it so hard to watch him go? Was it because she regretted misjudging him for so long? Was it because she just witnessed his act of bravery in the courtroom, and that somehow made it all worse?

Or was it because deep down, somewhere in her heart, there was a space only for him? There was a spot that he filled after all of her visits to his dilapidated house, all of his attempts to convince Oliver to give paw. Some part of her heart opened to him, and it appeared to be a much bigger part than she realized. As she watched him walk away, she could feel the ache of his absence deep in her chest.

She stood there feeling hollow. Her Wild West adventure was supposed to be fun. How did it feel like she'd lost everything now?

Chapter 25

Though he hated to leave Kayla standing there, Mitch knew that the plane was waiting for him and that he was already two hours behind the FBI agents who flew out to apprehend George. He thought about telling her that he was going to find Oliver, but he didn't want to get her hopes up in case he was unsuccessful. So instead, he just stood there and said nothing, as was his usual.

He tried to push it out of his mind. At least the testimony seemed to go well, and his father looked healthy. His duty was finally done, and the defense failed to make him look like some crazed, angry son.

Of course he was angry at his father for hurting so many people, but he wasn't out for revenge. He just wanted the scheming to stop. He wanted people to stop getting hurt.

That was another thing that he could've told Kayla. Instead of standing there and staring at her, he could've said, "Hey Kayla, guess what! I took your advice and I'll be using my dad's money for good."

He could've asked her to help, he could've told her that she was right all along. But no. He just stood there like a silent buffoon, as usual.

He was ready for the testimony and tough questions from the defense attorney. What he wasn't ready for was seeing her – that was a total surprise.

The Marshals escorted him onto the plane and gave him an update. Apparently, they were giving no warning that they were arriving to apprehend George. He would be taken completely by surprise. Mitch settled in for the flight and actually fell asleep a few minutes in. He awoke as the plane landed.

Agent Simmons was waiting on the tarmac. "Glad you made it," he said.

"Me too." Mitch got into the backseat of the SUV.

"I hope your testimony went okay?"

Mitch nodded. "It went well. I think."

"Perez thought so. Anyway," Simmons continued, "we've got George. We're questioning him now."

Mitch turned to him. "That's great. And Oliver?"

Agent Simmons shook his head. "No sign of him. And George seems to think he can use the dog as a bargaining chip."

Mitch realized that his hand was in a tight fist. He loosened it. "Can I talk to him?"

Simmons shook his head. "Sorry, no. Do you really think you'll do a better job interrogating him than someone that's trained for years on interrogation?"

"No, of course not," Mitch replied. "But I'd like a chance to at least scare him a little."

Simmons laughed. "We're waiting on a warrant to search his living quarters."

"How long will that take?"

"Unfortunately, it could take a few days."

"What?" Mitch sat up, trying to get closer to the front of the SUV. "Oliver could starve to death in that time."

"Listen, you've had a long day. Let me drop you off, we got a room for you at the farm where George was going to work."

Mitch was formulating his rebuttal when he realized what he just heard. "And George...he was staying at a house on the property?"

Simmons smiled. "He was. The house right next to the barn."

"Yeah," Mitch said. "I think I'm ready to turn in for the night."

They arrived not long after that, and Simmons wished him a good night. Mitch waved as the car drove away.

Clearly, Simmons was hinting for Mitch to take matters into his own hands. Normally, Mitch would be offended by something like this, saying that he wasn't like his father and wasn't going to break the law. Oddly though, right now he had no problem with a little breaking and entering.

There were several people milling about the property, but Mitch was able to find the house easily and without being noticed. The front door was locked, but the back door wasn't. Did it count as breaking and entering if the door wasn't locked?

He stepped inside and called out Oliver's name. Nothing. It wasn't a large house, and he searched room to room to find any clues of where Oliver may be.

There was nothing. No dog bowls, toys, or leash in sight. Was George really heartless enough to just leave Oliver in the wilderness somewhere to fend for himself?

Mitch unlocked the front door and took a seat on the swing on the front porch. He felt sick imagining that Oliver was hurt. He had the urge to call Simmons and demand that he be allowed to see George. While the professional interrogator probably had great skills, he wasn't allowed to physically drag George into the hallway to demand information about Oliver.

Mitch, however, would be happy to fill that role.

He stood up from the swing and accidentally knocked over the rake leaning against the railing. That wasn't a good place to keep such a big rake, he thought.

It dawned on him – there was no way that this farm kept its tools lying around like this. George must've gotten it from somewhere. But where?

There were two structures near the house. The first was the barn. Mitch went inside, peeking around corners and stalls to see if there was any sign of Oliver. He called his name with no response. He exited through the back door of the barn to see a smaller structure a few hundred yards away. It looked like a shed, just big enough to keep some tools and supplies.

He wanted to run but didn't want to raise any suspicion from the people hanging out. So he walked as quickly as he could, rake in hand, to the shed. The front door was closed and sealed with a padlock.

"Oliver!" He yelled. "Are you there boy?"

Silence. He pulled on the lock, hoping it would open on its own. It didn't budge, but he thought he heard something move inside of the shed.

"Oliver! Ollie!"

A bark rang out and Mitch felt his heart leap. It was him, it was definitely him.

Without thinking, he ran back up to the barn. He remembered seeing a pair of bolt cutters next to a muck fork. He grabbed it and jogged back to the shed. With one swift action, he cut the lock off and carefully opened the door.

Inside it was dark and quiet. Mitch squatted down, giving his eyes a second to adjust to the darkness.

"Ollie?"

Oliver poked his head out from behind a cardboard box. He approached slowly, tail tucked between his legs. Mitch was relieved to see that he looked unharmed.

"Hey buddy. It's okay, you're a good boy. You wanna go home? You wanna see Kayla?"

With the mention of her name, his entire expression changed. His ears perked up and he broke out of his creeping position. He wagged his tail and trotted over to Mitch, licking his hand over and over.

Mitch laughed. "That's the word, huh? Come on boy, let's go see Kayla. She's been looking all over for you."

Oliver followed him out of the shed and up the hill.

Chapter 26

After Mitch left, Kayla wasn't sure what to do with herself. What did she expect to happen? She listened to that kooky Silver guy who told her that she better be at the trial – and what? For what reason? She hardly got to see Mitch, and she didn't really get to talk to him.

Was this the end of her adventure? She was supposed to learn to say yes to new challenges, she was supposed to change her life. It didn't go as planned.

All she had left was a broken heart. She lost her dog to a scoundrel, made a fool of herself flirting with said scoundrel, and missed the great guy right in front of her the entire time.

She drove back to her apartment, feeling dejected.

When she got home, she made arrangements to fly back to Cody to continue her search for Oliver. She didn't have to return to work for another week, and she wanted to dedicate all the time that she could to finding him. She also needed to get back to Cody to transfer all of the money over to the Singers. The last time she checked, there was over $400,000 donated to their cause. It was a comfort to know that at least she was able to accomplish one good thing over the last few weeks.

She went to bed late that night, unable to fall asleep because she was looping over everything that happened in her mind. The next morning she awoke groggy and grumpy. It took her almost an hour to notice that she had a text message from an unknown number.

"Hey, I have some good news. Oliver is coming home today."

When she first read it, she thought it was some sort of a cruel prank. Something George would've dreamed up to torture her. Trying to keep from getting her hopes up, she responded, "Who is this?"

In response, she received a picture. It was Oliver, sitting happily on the seat of what appeared to be a plane, wearing a familiar looking cowboy hat. If she didn't know any better, she would think that it was Mitch's hat.

How could it be possible? Did Mitch really find him?

Her answer came not fifteen minutes later with a knock at the door. She ran over and practically flung the door open.

There stood Mitch with Oliver at his heel.

"Oliver!" she yelled. "I've missed you so much!"

Oliver didn't hesitate – he ran into the apartment, spinning in circles and licking her each time that he went around. Unable to contain his excitement, he let out a hybrid whimper bark. After about ten spins, he accidentally knocked Kayla over. Excited that she was finally down to his level, he hovered over her and licked her face while she squealed.

After a few minutes of this, Kayla managed to pull herself up from the ground. Her face was covered in slobber and tears, and her cheeks hurt from smiling so hard.

"Mitch," she said, "I'm so sorry to be rude, please come in."

"Thanks," he replied, grinning.

He stepped inside and she closed the door behind him. Oliver did his customary home inspection, trotting into the next room, sniffing briefly before running back to Kayla with a sigh.

"It looks like he's checking the place for security weaknesses," she said.

Mitch smiled. "Agent Oliver identified your first problem – your doorbell. Lets the bad guys say that they're here."

She laughed. "Definitely. He hates doorbells. And he's only ever heard them from TV. I'll need to get mine removed now that he's moved in."

"Seems like a good idea."

"I can't believe this," she said, kneeling to pet him. "Did George have him? What did he do to him?"

Mitch frowned. "Yeah, he had him. As far as I can tell, he thought he could use Oliver to get himself out of some trouble. He must've known that eventually he'd get caught. I don't think he harmed him, but he kept him locked in a shed. Or at least that's where I found him."

Poor Ollie must've been terrified, locked in a dark shed. Kayla felt anger wash over her. As his words sunk in, she realized what he'd just said. "Wait, *you* found Ollie? Not the FBI?"

"It's a long story. It was kind of a team effort."

Kayla felt the dog slobber drying on her face. It smelled terrible and she needed to wash it off, but she wanted to hear this story. "How about I go and wash some of these dog kisses off, and then you can tell me about it?"

"Sure," he responded. "Take your time."

Kayla, with Oliver close behind, quickly scooted into her bedroom and shut the door. She caught a horrifying glimpse of herself in the mirror – her hair piled on the top of her head in a disheveled bun, her face was all red, and she was still wearing her pajamas. This was not how she wanted Mitch to see her, especially if this might be the last time that she ever got to see him.

She went to the bathroom, washing her face and combing out her hair. After quietly turning on her hair straightener, she ran into the bedroom to throw on some halfway decent clothing. Most of her good outfits were still in Cody, unfortunately. It took a few minutes to tame her hair into somewhat reasonable shape, and she burned her finger in her haste.

Mitch had to wait precisely seven minutes – Kayla knew that because she kept a careful eye on the time.

"Sorry about that," she said sheepishly. "I wasn't quite ready for guests."

He stood up abruptly. "I'm so sorry, I can get out of your hair and let you –"

"No!" She said quickly. Wait – was he making fun of her hair? She decided not to think about it. "I'm fine now. I'd really like to hear about how you found Oliver. Would you like some tea?"

Kayla put on water for tea and spent the next half hour listening to Mitch. She realized that she never heard him talk for this long uninterrupted before – mostly because she was always interrupting him.

As much as he tried to downplay it, he was clearly the reason that Oliver was home safe. He refused to testify unless they found George, and when they found George, Mitch set out to see him immediately.

"I never took you for one to break the law," Kayla said with a smile after hearing about Agent Simmons' hint.

He laughed. "What do you mean? My father is a criminal. Like father, like son."

She scoffed. "Except your father wanted to make billions of dollars, and you wanted to save one yellow dog."

He looked up from his tea. "Is there much of a difference between the two?"

"Not to me," she said. "Except I prefer the dog to the billions of dollars."

"That's a shame," he said. "Because I decided to finally take your advice. You're looking at New York State's newest billionaire."

"Shut up!" she blurted out without thinking.

He crossed his arms and his cheeks seemed to flush a little. "I'm sorry, but it's the truth. It just took me some time to realize that you were right."

"Did you hear that Ollie? I was right about something!"

Mitch stooped down to pat Oliver on the back. "Now don't you go teaching him how to gloat, he already is a bit too smug when he's supposed to bring his ball back for fetch."

"You're right," Kayla replied, feigning seriousness. "I'm sorry."

They sat for a moment in what was definitely an awkward silence. As much as Kayla wanted Mitch to accept the money, part of her never really believed that he would. And now, sitting across from her dog's billionaire rescuer, she didn't know what to say. It was almost as though she felt shy for a moment.

But she had to fill the silence. "So are you still going to live in Cody?"

He shrugged. "I'm not sure yet. If I'm going to spend my days funding worthy charities, I might need to spend some time in some bigger cities. I do love Cody, though. I think my first exorbitant purchase will be a little jet of my own."

She narrowed her eyes at him. "I never took you as a man who liked luxury. Have I created a monster?"

He laughed. "I don't think you have to worry about that. As much as I like the convenience, mostly I like the safety."

"But I thought all of the guys who are out to get us are going to jail?"

Mitch nodded. "Probably all the ones coming after you will go to jail, but I may always be a target. I've decided to keep my fake name even though I've left the official witness protection program. I'll probably need to employ my own security for the rest of my life. It'll be a small expense, comparatively."

"I'm not surprised that you left the program," said Kayla with a dry tone. "Now that you're rich, you can't be forced to live in that shack the Marshals gave you."

"No, in fact, I should probably level it and start over."

They both laughed. She couldn't think of a single person who would be less spoiled by money. She was thinking of how to respond when her phone rang. "Sorry about this, it's my mom, one second."

"Take your time," he said.

Kayla answered the call. Her mom wanted to remind her that she agreed to come over for lunch before her flight back to Cody.

"Well Mom, I've got some good news. I have Oliver back…" She was interrupted by her mom's squeals and slew of questions.

"Yes, I'll still come over for lunch. Okay, I know." Kayla sighed impatiently. "I told you, I'll pick some up on the way."

She closed her eyes. For some reason, Mitch seeing her barely able to get a word in was mortifying. It took her a few minutes for her to convince her mom that she would remember to bring over tortilla chips, as promised.

"I'm sorry about that," said Kayla after she hung up.

Mitch stood and carried his tea mug over to the sink. "No, it's time for me to get going anyways. It was nice seeing you again. Let me know if you ever need anything?"

Kayla forced herself to smile. "Yeah, of course. You too. And I didn't get to thank you properly before, but...thank you so much for everything. For saving Oliver, and for saving me from being kidnapped."

Mitch paused, looking deeply into her eyes for a moment. She felt her heart skip a beat.

"It was the least I could do," he said. "But you're welcome. Have a good rest of your day."

The moment passed. He turned to walk to her front door.

"Thanks, you too," she said lamely.

Kayla opened the door for him and watched him walk to his truck. He got inside and waved goodbye before he pulled away.

After she closed the door, she stood there for a moment. It was like a hurricane just blew through or something. She felt off.

She was thrilled to have Oliver back, and Mitch behaved rather heroically in finding him. Never in a million years did she think that he would break the law for any reason. Clearly, she was wrong in thinking that he was angry at her. Yet she was clearly also wrong in thinking that he liked her.

At least she had his phone number now in case she had any needs for a low key burglary or bankrolling another fundraiser.

Somehow none of that seemed like much of a consolation. She was going to miss him terribly.

Oliver hopped onto the couch and then stared at Kayla with a guilty look on his face. When she approached him, he started slowly wagging his tail, as though he was asking if his move to the couch was allowed.

"Oh it's okay. You're a good boy." She stroked his head and he perked up. "We've been on quite an adventure, haven't we boy? I guess it wasn't all bad."

Oliver took a satisfied breath before rolling over to expose his belly. Kayla sat next to him and obliged him with some belly rubs.

There was a knock at the door. Ollie leapt from the couch, barking ferociously. Kayla's heart rate shot up – who could that be? Maybe she wasn't entirely safe from the goons after all.

She strained her neck looking out of the side of the window to see who it was. It looked like Mitch. He must've forgotten something.

"Hey, what's up?" she asked as she opened the door.

"Uh –" He was somewhat breathless, staring at her with his mouth open.

She scrunched her eyebrows. "Are you okay? Come on Mitch, use your words. Is someone after you?"

"No, everything's fine," he said. He took a deep breath. "I just forgot to tell you something. Silver said something to me that made it sound like you thought I was angry with you. I was never angry with you, just worried."

"Oh," she said, "I know. And I'm so thankful for everything. Just that – you know, for everything you did for Oliver. And my mom and dad wanted to thank you too."

He took a step towards her. "You must know, everything I did – with Silver, with Oliver – it was all for you. I love you," he blurted out. "And I have for a long time. I don't expect anything from you – but I couldn't live with myself if you didn't know."

Kayla stood in her doorway, mouth hanging open.

He smiled. "Okay, well, uh, see you later."

Mitch turned to leave; he was halfway to his car before Kayla realized what was going on and ran after him.

"Wait!" she called out. "Don't go yet!"

He stopped and turned towards her.

She had to think of something. "You don't even know my real name!"

He gave her a puzzled look and they both burst into laughter.

"Well, what is it?" he asked.

"It's Alex. Alexandra Small."

He took a step closer to her. "Well Alex, it's very nice to meet you."

"And I love you too," she said breathlessly. "I'm so sorry about all of the – "

In that moment, his lips met hers. It felt like a jolt ran through her chest. She threw her arms around his neck and kissed him back.

He was an amazing kisser.

It made sense that he would be. All evidence pointed to those strong, silent types being better with actions than words.

Epilogue

Her last patient of the day was Mrs. Higgins; she was the picture of health, as usual, and the appointment finished five minutes early.

"Now you make sure to take some of these cookies to that husband of yours," Mrs. Higgins said sternly. "I heard that last time he didn't get a single one!"

Alex laughed. "Only because the girls ate them all! But I'll make sure to sneak him a few."

"Good," she responded, satisfied.

Mrs. Higgins always demanded to see pictures of Mitch so she could coo and say, "What a handsome young man! You're going to have beautiful babies."

Alex always smiled and thanked her. She didn't tell any of her patients – or anyone, for that matter – that they started trying to conceive as soon as they were married. It wasn't an easy thing for her to talk about because they hadn't had any luck. Alex hoped that their luck was about to change.

She left the clinic in a rush to make it to her doctor's appointment. Mitch was going to meet her there – he was flying in from New York City after attending a meeting to discuss funding allocation for some of their charities.

Despite hurrying the whole way there, Alex made it to the clinic two minutes late. She felt bad about being late and told the receptionist that she was sorry several times. After checking in, she sat in the waiting room for 15 minutes before being called back to a room. At least Mitch was later than she was, she reasoned.

The nurse took her weight and blood pressure, then gave her a gown to change into. Mitch came in not long after, concerned that he missed the doctor.

"Don't worry," she said. "They're running even later than both of us."

"That's a relief," he replied.

After a few minutes, Dr. Choi knocked gently on the door.

"So I heard that we might have some good news?" she said, shaking both of their hands.

Alex looked at Mitch, then back to the doctor. "I hope so."

Dr. Choi turned to her computer and clicked around for a moment. "Well, your hCG levels are rising. That's a *very* good sign."

Alex squeezed Mitch's hand but said nothing.

"Shall we have a look? I'll get our ultrasound technician Brenda to come in."

Alex held her breath. She still didn't believe it to be true. Not yet at least.

Brenda came into the room, introduced herself and squirted some gel onto Alex's abdomen. She expected it to be cold, but apparently they kept it in some sort of a warmer. How fancy.

Brenda gently pressed the wand gently against Alex's stomach. "All right...do you see that there?"

Alex and Mitch simultaneously leaned in.

"I think so!" said Alex

"That," said Brenda with a smile, "is your baby."

Alex immediately burst into tears. For some reason, she couldn't allow herself to believe that this pregnancy was real until that moment.

After a few minutes, she regained her composure. Mitch held her hand throughout, and when she looked up at him, she saw that his eyes were brimming with tears.

They received the due date and instructions for the next visit, but Alex was hardly listening. Now she knew how her patients felt when she talked too much during appointments. It was just too much to take in all at once.

She felt like her body was laying there, under the ultrasound wand, but her soul was floating at the top of the room, about to break through the ceiling tiles, through the roof, and into the clouds.

After the appointment, she still felt like she was drifting on a cloud. She and Mitch walked back to his old truck in silence.

He opened the passenger side door for her, helping her into the truck. He always did that. She thought he might stop after they were dating for a while, and then after they were married. But he insisted on it, and though she liked to tease him any chance she got, she'd never complain about that.

"Well," he said as he climbed into the driver's seat. "I thought I would never be happier than the day that you told me you loved me. And then I thought I would never be happier than the day that I got to marry you. But somehow, you keep outdoing yourself."

Alex smiled, still too dazed to think clearly.

"You're welcome," she said.

He chuckled and pulled her in for a hug.

"It was all for the money," she said, her voice muffled. "I never would've had you otherwise."

He pulled away, eying her suspiciously. "Uh huh. I knew that was what you were after all along."

She grabbed the sides of his face and pulled him in, planting a hard kiss on his cheek. That was a joke they could only do in private, because they tried to keep Mitch's billions under wraps. After all, he planned to have most of it given away over the next decade.

"You're the poorest billionaire I know, Mitch Aiken. But I love you all the same."

He returned a delicate kiss on her cheek before starting the car. "How are we gonna break the news?"

Alex raised an eyebrow. "To our families?"

He waved a hand. "No, not them. They're easy. I mean how are we going to tell Oliver that he's going to be a big brother?"

"Oh dear," she said, shaking her head. "He's not going to get an ounce of sleep with this new baby human to protect."

Mitch started the car. "Well, a dog's duty is never done. He has to guard us at all times. That's how he earns his keep."

"That's right," Alex added, trying to be serious. It didn't work and she cracked a smile. "I think Oliver will probably be the most dedicated special agent that our baby will ever know."

He took her hand. "I think you're right."

She sighed deeply, enjoying the moment. Her stomach let out a loud growl.

Mitch looked over at her, a horrified look on his face. "Was that you?"

"Yeah! You're keeping a pregnant woman waiting for dinner! What are you thinking?"

"Very sorry ma'am," he said, speeding up the truck. "Where would you like to go?"

She tapped her chin. "Take me out for pizza again. Like we did for our first date when you couldn't talk to me."

He smiled. "Done. But I can't promise that I can keep my mouth shut this time."

"That's okay," she said. "I kind of like talking to you now."

"Is that right?"

She nodded. "It is."

"Does that mean you're going to listen to me, then?"

She laughed. "Don't push your luck, buddy."

Author's Note

Thanks for reading! I'd love to know what you thought, and reader reviews are one of the most influential factors in whether someone will give a book a chance. So, if you've enjoyed this book, would you please consider reviewing it?

Would you like my free novella?

Sign up for my newsletter and get a copy of my free novella "Falling for my Brother's Billionaire Best Friend." I use my newsletter to send updates about new releases and sales! Oh, and to tell embarrassing stories about my husband. You can sign up by visiting: http://bit.ly/ameliastory

Introduction to *Veterinarian's Date with a Billionaire*
by Amelia Addler

She needs to save her veterinary clinic. He needs to win her back. An impromptu road trip might be just what the doctor ordered.

Juliet's in trouble. Not only is her low-cost clinic running out of money, she's also flat broke. When she enters a competition to save the clinic, she doesn't expect her car to break down and ruin her plans. She also doesn't expect her charming ex-boyfriend James to appear out of nowhere and insist on chauffeuring her around.

James can't believe his good luck. He returned to his hometown to win Juliet back and almost immediately gets to come to her rescue. It's exactly what he needs to show her that he'll do anything to make up for his past mistakes.

Will Juliet's theory of "never forgive or forget" be proven right? Or did heartbreak force James to become the better man that she needed?

Veterinarian's Date with a Billionaire, a second chance romance, is part of the "Billionaire Date Book" series, but can be read as a standalone story. Not intended for audiences who don't like smart heroines, love-struck billionaires, or cute animals. For everyone else: enjoy!

Excerpt follows:

Chapter 1

It didn't take long for Juliet to spot her friends laughing in a booth at the far corner of the restaurant. They didn't see her coming. A smile spread across her face as she walked toward them.

"Well, well, well," she said, arms crossed. "If it isn't the Dynamic Duo of Wayside High School."

"No," Greg replied, standing from his seat. "With you, we're the Three Stooges."

Juliet broke into laughter. "I completely forgot that they used to call us that." She pulled Greg in for a hug.

Aaron stood up, wrapping his arms around them both in a group hug.

"When did you get so strong?" squeaked Juliet.

Aaron shrugged. "I have to be able to hold a wriggling four-year-old twin in each arm, and I think that's the ultimate workout."

"Oh my gosh, I haven't gotten to see them since their third birthday party. I haven't seen you guys in forever!" said Juliet as she took a seat.

Greg shook his head. "No, that's not true. We all hung out six months ago, at my wedding. And my bachelor party, though the kids weren't there."

"Ah, of course. How could I forget?"

How *could* she forget? She was the only woman invited on the bachelor party – a four day backpacking trip in the mountains. She was worried that she wouldn't be able to keep up, but she was one of the fastest in the pack. It seemed that getting married and having kids really slowed the rest of her friends down.

"So Jules," said Greg, "What's this project that you need help with?"

She took a deep breath. "It's a long story, but basically, the vet clinic where I work is at risk of being shut down."

They looked at her with surprise, and she was about to continue when something caught her eye. It looked like...but no, it couldn't be.

Greg turned around to see what she was squinting at. "What?"

"Shh!" She kicked him under the table. "Turn around!"

Greg snapped back to face her just as Aaron leaned across the table to see what was so interesting.

"Could you guys be any more obvious? I thought I saw someone, but – it turns out I was wrong."

Aaron shrugged. "It's the Wednesday before Thanksgiving. We probably know everybody in this restaurant. It's practically a high school reunion."

Juliet cautioned a glance toward the front door again. She was being silly; there was no one there and she'd gotten all flustered for nothing.

She cleared her throat and started again. "We had grant funding from – "

A voice cut her off from behind. "Hey guys! How's it going?"

Her eyes didn't deceive her. She'd know that voice anywhere: her ex-boyfriend, James Balin.

"Hey man! Long time no see. How's it going?" Greg offered a handshake before motioning for James to take a seat.

That flushed feeling was back, and Juliet knew that the skin on her chest was bright red under her hoodie. This was the *last* thing she thought she'd have to face during this visit to her hometown.

Her mom nagging her about her hair being too long? Yes, always. The owner of the restaurant scolding her, for the thousandth time, about breaking a huge stack of dishes back when she was a freshman in high school? Sure.

But running into James? Definitely not. As far as she knew, he hadn't been back to Michigan in years. His family didn't even live there anymore. It made her feel a little rattled to see him appear like that. But she didn't want him thinking that he could rattle her, so she needed to play it cool.

Juliet turned to him and smiled with as much grace as she could muster. He hadn't aged a day – well, not in a normal way, more like a George Clooney way. His blue eyes were as bright as ever, and she had to force herself not to stare. James had many flaws, but being homely was not one of them.

"Pretty good, it's good to see you all," James said. His eyes met Juliet's. "Do you mind if I join you?"

Before she could think of an excuse as to why he couldn't sit with them, Aaron said, "No, of course not!"

She reminded herself to breathe slowly. This was the problem with having guy friends. It was all fine and dandy until an ex-boyfriend showed up. If Juliet's female friends were there, they would've known that the ex-boyfriend protocol called for civility with a large helping of coldness.

They wouldn't shake his hand. They wouldn't ask how he was doing – unless they planned to look away, disinterested in his answer. And they certainly wouldn't have invited him to sit down!

James scooted into the booth next to Greg.

"Hi James, fancy seeing you here," she said coolly.

"Yeah, I'm in town, kinda a surprise actually. Zach invites me for Thanksgiving every year, and I finally took him up on it."

Juliet shifted uncomfortably to make sure her legs didn't brush against his; there wasn't enough room in the booth for another person.

"Oh yeah? How's he doing?" asked Aaron.

"Really well," replied James. "I haven't been able to see him for a while, so it's a nice treat."

Juliet had to force herself not to say something snarky back to him, like "I'm sure it is hard to see your best friend when you refuse to leave your precious New York City."

Instead, she said, "Is your dad alone for Thanksgiving?"

James laughed. "No, he's got all of his coworkers to keep him company. They're working on a big presentation for some investors, I doubt they'll take any breaks for Thanksgiving dinner. Or Christmas."

"I see."

"It's so nice to see you Juliet, I can't believe I ran into you here," said James.

What was he going on about? Where else would she be for Thanksgiving? Oh – yeah, she could be with her boyfriend's family. If she had a boyfriend.

"Yeah, it's nice to see you too," she lied.

Greg prompted her again. "So what's going on with the clinic?"

"Oh!" James said, eyes lighting up. "Are you working at a clinic here?"

"Westside Veterinary Clinic," she said, keeping the edge out of her tone. "In Lansing."

It was best to remain neutral, she decided. She'd carry on as though he wasn't even there, or as though it wasn't the first time she'd seen him in five years. It'd been so long that it was just like seeing a stranger. At least that's what she told herself to keep from getting frazzled.

"We got notice two months ago that our funding will run out at the end of the year, and it won't be renewed. The grant agency is no longer able to fund vet clinics."

Aaron shook his head. "That's awful. How long can the clinic survive without funding?"

Juliet sighed. "A month? Maybe two? Not very long. We don't make much profit, because everything we do is offered on a sliding scale based on people's income. It's not enough to cover operating costs – hence why we got the grant for being a vet clinic in an under-served area."

"That's so nice though," interjected James. "You're helping, uh, poor people take care of their pets?"

She turned to him with the slightest glare in her eye. "When you say it like that you make them sound like they're homeless. They just don't have a lot of extra money to spend on their pets. But it doesn't mean that they love them any less."

"Of course not," James added, shaking his head.

Juliet turned back to her friends. "But I came up with a plan. There is this newish company that develops cancer drugs. They're not huge, but one of their drugs has been out for years. At first, it was only available for use in animals, but now it's undergoing human trials. They're holding a contest to raise awareness for how well the drug works. The winner of the contest will get one million dollars for a veterinary clinic, plus a stipend to run clinical trials."

Aaron raised his eyebrows. "That's incredible. What's in it for them?"

"Well, they want people to put together a video of animals that were saved by the drug. They're going to use that for marketing and fundraising, I don't know."

James nodded. "It's actually really smart. This can create a lot of hype, even beyond the winning video. It'll help them with investment and buy in, more than a million dollars in advertising could do alone."

Before Juliet had the chance to cut him off, Aaron asked, "Does your dad's company have something like that?"

James shook his head. "No, we have an in-house marketing department who spends *plenty* of money on their own. Plus, none of the drugs that we developed are used in animals, just in people. But it's not a bad idea."

"Anyways," Juliet said, "I contacted a lot of my old vet school friends who are at some of the bigger veterinary practices. They've been using this drug for years and some of their patients agreed to appear in a video about it. Which is where I come in. I'm going to make this video and win the contest. I hope."

Greg smiled and patted the dark bag sitting on the table. "I brought my old camera, just like you asked. It's all yours."

Aaron leaned back, crossing his arms. "And Greg is going to edit this video for you, right?"

Juliet shrugged, a smile on her lips. "No, I can't afford to pay him."

Greg laughed. "Oh, please. It would be nice to edit something other than wedding videos for once. And it's an honor to loan my skills to your vet clinic for poor people."

Juliet had to swallow to suppress the laugh that almost sprung from her chest. Maybe guy friends had *some* merits.

"Thanks Greg, that means a lot," said Juliet.

"I know a good bit about how drug companies work," James said, apparently missing Greg's jab at him. "Maybe I could be of some help?"

"I think I'll be okay," replied Juliet.

She was unable to force herself to smile this time. Why did James think he could show up in town after all these years and act like he was just another member of the gang? Did he think that she'd look at him and want to be friends all of a sudden?

Luckily, at that moment, Zach came over to their table. "Hey guys, good to see you."

Everyone smiled and said their hello's. Juliet made a point of being much warmer to Zach than she was to James. She liked Zach, after all. It wasn't his fault that his best friend was a jerk.

"James – we're going to put our dinner orders in soon. Do you want to come over or...?"

"Oh, of course. Sorry, sure." James stood from the table. "It was really nice catching up with you guys. Maybe I'll see you later?"

"Sure, see you later," said Aaron.

Juliet waited until they were out of earshot to speak again. "Thanks a lot guys," she hissed. "I really wanted to have to pretend to be nice to my ex-boyfriend."

Greg and Aaron started laughing.

"What's so funny?" she said, deciding again that guy friends were no good.

"I don't think that anyone would think that you were trying to be nice to him."

She crossed her arms. "What's that supposed to mean? And why did you tell him to sit down?"

Greg shrugged. "I didn't want to be rude. And besides, it's been a long time. Maybe it's time for you to forgive? You can forgive but not forget."

"You know I hate that phrase."

"Yeah, we know," Aaron said with a grin. "Maybe it's time to get over it?"

"No! It's a stupid phrase! If you forgive, but you still hang onto whatever they did, then that's not really forgiveness, is it?"

Greg shrugged. "I mean, it's a form of forgiveness."

"No, it's not forgiveness," Juliet said matter-of-factly.

"Okay then, just forgive and forget," said Aaron.

Juliet realized that her shoulders were scrunched halfway up to her ears. She released the tension. "There are some things that can't be forgiven."

Aaron and Greg looked at each other, then back at Juliet.

"You're still *that* mad?" asked Aaron. "I don't think that's good for your health."

Greg tried to hide his smile behind a menu.

She wasn't going to play into their teasing anymore. "I'm not mad. I just keep a very updated list of people to be avoided."

"Like a black book with people you hate?" asked Greg.

Juliet sighed. "No, I don't 'hate' anybody. There are just certain people that you can never trust."

Aaron got a very serious look on his face. "We better be careful, or we'll end up on her list."

Greg nodded. "It's kinda like a Do Not Call list. But it's worse – a Do Not Trust list."

Juliet threw a sugar packet at him. "You're both going to end up on my Do Not Call list soon."

They laughed and finally moved onto another topic.

The rest of the evening was nice, even though Juliet felt like her nerves were on edge. She constantly looked to see if James was going to sneak up on them again. Luckily, he didn't, and after they paid their tab, they walked out to the parking lot together without any sign of James.

Aaron made them all promise to stop by his house after Thanksgiving dinner, and they agreed. Juliet waved goodbye, still on alert that James could show up at any minute. She quickly started her car and was about to pull away from her parking spot when the car suddenly stopped.

"What in the world?"

She tried turning the key in the ignition again, but that didn't do anything. She put her foot on the gas with no response. She realized that everything in the car was dark – even the clock stopped glowing. She pulled the emergency brake and got out to take a look at it.

Greg and Aaron were still chatting and came over to see what was going on.

"What happened?" asked Greg.

"I have no idea. It was going, and then all of a sudden, it wasn't."

"Maybe I could take a look?" said a new voice.

Juliet closed her eyes. Of course James found her again. Just when she was about to get away from him for good.

Chapter 2

James took a step forward and opened the hood of Juliet's Saturn Vue. He didn't know much about cars, so he wasn't really sure what he was looking at, but he still wanted to try. He would do anything for a chance to talk to Juliet for just a bit longer.

Luckily for him, Aaron took the lead with the car. "Well, your oil looks okay. I don't see anything obviously wrong, but Juliet, this is a pretty old car. It might be the engine or the transmission."

She put her hands on her hips. "It can't be broken right now. Why couldn't it break *next* week? I have to drive to Ann Arbor on Friday – it was the only day the lady with the parrot could meet."

James saw his chance. "I have the whole week off. I could drive you anywhere you need to go."

She responded without looking at him. "Thanks, but I'm sure my car just needs some type of fluid or something and it'll be back up and running."

"I'm not sure about that Jules," Greg said, shifting his weight. "And you're gonna have a hard time finding a car to rent the day after Thanksgiving."

James tried to suppress a smile. Clearly Greg didn't hold a grudge as long as Juliet did.

"It wouldn't be the worst thing for you to have someone go with you," Aaron added. "You don't know the people you're going to meet. What if one of them attacks you or something?"

"Why would anyone attack me? I'm sure they're all nice, normal people. Since when are you so paranoid?"

Greg shrugged. "Better safe than sorry, don't you think?"

A vein bulged from Juliet's forehead, but she didn't respond. She got back into the driver's seat and turned her key in the ignition again. The car didn't even try to start.

James felt almost giddy with excitement.

"I can give you a ride back to your parents' house if you like," he said.

"No thank you," she responded. "Greg – their house is on your way home. You don't mind, do you?"

"No, of course not. Let's go."

"My offer to drive you on Friday stands!" James yelled after her. "You still have my number, right?"

"No, I deleted it," she shouted without looking back.

He frowned. This wasn't going to be easy, but he knew that when he made the decision to come back to Michigan. "I'll text you so you can let me know if you need my help."

She got into the passenger seat of Greg's car without responding. James watched as they pulled away.

Although it wasn't exactly a warm welcome, it was still a better interaction than he expected. Juliet was a tough cookie – it was one of the things he loved most about her.

Yet it wasn't easy for him to face her. He couldn't go a day without thinking of her, but he was afraid of her, too. So instead of doing the brave thing and telling her how he felt, he found ways to distract himself.

His job was one of the few things that could keep his mind occupied. It worked – for a while, at least. He never allowed himself to take a break. He knew that taking a break would mean he'd have time to think, and if he had time to think, loneliness and regret would engulf him. One year, he spent so much time traveling and meeting investors that he spent a total of three weeks at home.

He could feel himself growing thin, but he *couldn't* stop. Instead, he started slipping at work. His presentations got sloppy. He forgot to send in orders. His father was perpetually disappointed with him, at one point dubbing him a "brainless wonder" who needed to be "studied for the good of humanity."

That was a *bit* harsh. It all started eating away at James, and everything came to a head the week before Thanksgiving. He was supposed to meet with one of their oldest investors to give them an update on the company's metrics. It wasn't a huge challenge, but the pressure was intense. Losing the investor could endanger the company – a fact that his dad made sure to tell him when he reminded him to "pack a brain" for the trip.

So naturally, James stayed up too late the night before the meeting. He was anxious, burnt out and brittle. He couldn't fall asleep and ended up watching *The Great British Baking Show* for five straight episodes. The premise was delightful;

there was no competitive nastiness between the contestants and the bakers were so passionate. It was the opposite of his job.

The next day, he overslept and completely missed the meeting. When he showed up three hours late, he tried to sneak into the building, only to be escorted out by security.

Word got back to his dad rather quickly about what happened. James got to hear that he was a disappointment, a failure, and that he endangered the company and the jobs of everyone there. To James, it very much sounded like he was fired, which was problematic, because he was supposed to take over the company when his dad retired.

Yet somehow, when he thought me might be fired, he didn't feel upset. His heart soared. Being fired meant freedom. He no longer had to work at a job that he didn't care about and towards goals that meant nothing to him.

He knew that he couldn't work any harder, no matter how many rude nicknames his dad made up for him. The job made him unhappy – no, his own choices made him unhappy. The job was just one of them. James realized that he had to face the poor choices he'd made and try to undo them.

So instead of arguing with his dad, he decided to run away without another word between them.

Well – that wasn't exactly true. It wasn't *exactly* running away. He felt guilty for not seeing his best friend for over three years, so that was part of his decision to flee New York. Also, he could better wait out his father's temper tantrum by removing himself from the city.

But the real reason was more than that. Much more than that – it had to do with someone that popped into his mind whenever he went for a long run or woke up before his alarm. It was something that nagged him late at night and when he sat down to eat dinner alone.

Maybe his dad was right, and he was a failure and a "brainless wonder." James didn't know, and he didn't much care anymore. His own spectacular failure freed him from the need to be successful at work.

What he did know was that after five years, he still wasn't over Juliet. He knew that he would never be over her. It was the only thing he was sure of – Juliet McCarron was the love of his life. He took a wrong turn when he lost her and he would do anything to win her back.

And so far, it was going much better than he could have ever planned. Juliet was at the Two Rivers Grille, just like Zach said she would be. Of course, she looked *amazing*. She wasn't trying to, naturally – she was in a hooded sweatshirt, her long blonde hair pulled back into a loose ponytail – and it only added to her charm.

Sure, she wasn't thrilled to see him, but he expected that. James knew that she wouldn't welcome him with open arms. He hoped that maybe she'd missed him too, but her feigned indifference was okay. It wasn't Juliet's way to forgive easily. He fully intended to apologize for how he'd hurt her in the past, knowing that the hardest part would be getting her to talk to him in the first place.

It was unbelievably lucky that her car broke down. It was so brilliant that he worried that she may even accuse him of doing something to her car. He never would've done that – but he was thrilled that the universe offered him a helping hand in the matter anyway.

He pulled out his phone and found her in his list of contacts. How many times did he pull her name up, press CALL and then hang up? How many times did he have a message typed out, only to delete it?

Hopefully she hadn't changed her phone number since they last spoke – if so, he still knew the number for her parents' house.

He typed out a text message: "Hi Juliet, this is James with your free taxi service. We're running a special this week for the low cost of zero dollars. Please respond to this message if you are interested."

He hit send and smiled. That would crack her up, right?

Three hours later and no answer. He decided to send one more message. "Please also respond if you are not interested, as we have many parties creating inspiring veterinary videos in need of the service."

He stayed up late that night, hoping that she might write back. She did not.

James got up early the next morning and helped Zach's mom prepare for Thanksgiving dinner. Despite not coming to visit in years, she still treated him like he was family. He didn't have a single friend like that in New York, and he hated himself for not visiting for so long.

There were 24 people coming for dinner that evening, and that meant there was plenty of help needed. James was initially on potato peeling duty, but he was so slow that he was switched to setting up the tables and chairs. It was nice to catch up with Zach and to spend some quality time with Zach's wife Amy – even though Amy's favorite activity was teasing him mercilessly.

Dinner came and went without any response from Juliet. James decided to bring it up to Zach and Amy as they washed and dried dishes.

"Would it be weird if I showed up at her parents' house, just to say hello?"

Zach handed him a bowl to dry. "It would be weird, because you haven't been there in years, and you're not just stopping by to say hello."

James frowned. "True."

The last time that he spoke to Juliet was the night that she broke up with him and refused to speak to him again. He was surprised by the finality of her decision; things were great until that point.

Well, almost – their relationship was wonderful for the first two years when they were both in college. It did get a bit rocky when James graduated and moved to New York City; Juliet still had one year left at school, but he thought that they were strong enough to survive the distance.

James' excitement to start working at his dad's company clouded his judgement; he finally had a chance to prove himself and he didn't think that being apart would be *that* bad. Yet after he started working, their easy relationship became difficult; – there were arguments, tense silences, and a lack of understanding between them.

"What's inspiring you to show up at Juliet's house all of a sudden?" asked Amy.

"It's not quite all of a sudden," James replied. "I haven't stopped thinking about her since we broke up. She's the one that got away."

No matter who he met, no one measured up to her. Dating was tough, though he tried to give it a fair shot. Instead of focusing on whatever his date was telling him, he found himself wondering what Juliet was doing or what she would say about a new movie or TV show.

Though he tried not to, he compared every woman that he met to her. It didn't help that he kept attracting the wrong type of person – women who thought he was into the money, the job title, and the New York partying scene. He wasn't.

If there was a girl like Juliet in New York City, he couldn't find her. There was no one with her never-ending passion, no one with her sharp tongue and tender heart (that was covered with a thin, but hard, shell).

"Aw, that's kind of sweet. How long has it been?" asked Amy.

"A long time," said James. "Five years."

Zach let out a long whistle. "Wow, I did *not* realize that it was that long since you proposed to her."

"You proposed to her!" gasped Amy. "So you were engaged? I never knew that."

"No," James said, tugging at his collar. Was it getting hot in there from all the dish washing? "She turned me down. I made some selfish choices that pushed her away – especially in that last year we were together. There was one in particular that I'm still embarrassed about."

"Do tell," said Amy.

James shook his head. "Not today. I've already revealed enough embarrassing stuff. But I got pretty desperate, I could feel her slipping away, and I was too dumb to put two and two together. I thought all I needed to do was propose to show her how much I loved her."

"Yeah," interjected Zach. "Proposing was *not* the way to communicate your feelings. You should've *actually* communicated your feelings – using words. And not just the words, 'Will you marry me?' "

"So she said no?" Amy leaned back on the sink, taking a break from scrubbing the turkey pan. "And then for five years you didn't even try to talk to her?"

"Of course I tried to talk to her, but she never answered. Not once. So I wanted to respect her decision and try to move on. And then the time flew and...well, yeah, it was stupid. I thought I could get over her. I can't."

Part of the reason why time went so quickly was because James threw himself into his work. If he worked evenings and weekends and holidays, it helped keep his head clear. Also, the more hours he put in, the more that his dad was somewhat happy with him.

Clearly, after a year of Juliet not returning his messages, he should have changed his tactics. But he was afraid – if he actually went to her and asked for a second chance, she could reject him for the final time. If he never asked, the chance was always out there. At least that's what he told himself.

"And now you show up, hoping that Juliet won't be able to resist your cool car," Amy said with a smile.

"No." James laughed. Zach really married quite a firecracker. "In fact, she'd be more likely to agree to travel with me if I had a different car. Juliet is not into flashy stuff."

"Then why did you bring a flashy car here?" asked Zach.

"Well, my dad's kinda angry with me right now for a work related issue. He blocked my access to the garage, and he froze all of my work-related bank accounts and credit cards."

"Whoa," said Amy. "Your dad takes a family feud to the next level."

"He always has. He tells me that it's for my own good, and that if I expect to successfully run a multi-billion dollar company once he's gone, then I need some tough love."

"That's very tough love," said Amy. "I thought my parents were hard on me. All they ever did was send me to my room to think about what I'd done."

"Well," Zach said, "when your son has access to your billions of dollars, you can't really send him to his room. He might, oh, I don't know – fly off to Amsterdam or something. But definitely not to his room."

James rolled his eyes. "That was *one* time. And you loved that trip! You make me sound like a trust fund brat."

"I did love that trip, thanks again bud," Zach conceded. "But don't take this the wrong way. You kind of *are* a trust fund kid. Why don't you have your own bank account?"

"I do have my own bank account!" James protested. "He froze the other one."

Amy snorted. "The *other* one? You know the rest of us don't share bank accounts with our fathers."

"It's a company bank account. For expenses and stuff."

"Uh huh," Zach nodded. "Then how much money do you have in your real bank account? The one where your direct deposits go?"

"There's enough money in there to get by," he said with a frown.

He honestly had no idea. He'd never kept track of money – he didn't need to. James knew that meant he was spoiled, but what was he supposed to do? He wasn't going to turn away company money for company purposes. He barely even slept in his condo in New York because he was always working.

Zach laughed. "I know you don't even know how much money you have in there. I love you man, but that's not normal. And you *did* total your dad's Bentley."

James cringed. "True. But it's just a car. I don't know what he was so mad about."

He was only able to keep a straight face for five seconds before he burst out laughing.

"Okay, yeah, that was pretty bad. But he has like three other ones. And he's always mad at me for something. It doesn't matter what I do."

"Why don't you just talk to him?" said Amy. "It sounds like you guys have a lot of anger and not a lot of communication."

James took a stack of dishes and loaded them back into the cupboard. "It's hard. He's been very closed off since my mom died. He wants me to do well, but I don't know what that means, so he gets angry. And then I act out, and here we are."

"Stop being a big teenager," said Zach. "You guys have been fighting this way since you were 13."

"I know, but I'm not going to be the first one to budge," said James.

Amy snapped him with a towel.

"Ow! You're really good at that!"

"Listen to Zach!" she said. "One of you has to give in."

James felt his phone buzz in his pocket and reached to grab it. "Well it's not going to be me. Especially because my taxi service may have just gotten its first customer."

Veterinarian's Date with a Billionaire — available on Amazon now.

About the Author

Amelia Addler writes always clean, always swoon-worthy romance stories and believes that everyone deserves their own happily ever after.

Her soulmate is a man who once spent five weeks driving her to work at 4AM after her car broke down (and he didn't complain, not even once). She is lucky enough to be married to that man and they live in Pittsburgh with their little yellow mutt. Visit her website at AmeliaAddler.com or drop her an email at AmeliaAddler@gmail.com.

Also by Amelia...

The Westcott Bay Series

The Billionaire Date Book Series